WILD RIVER MASSACRE

WILD RIVER MASSACRE

Jack Curtis

GUNSMOKE

This hardback edition 2011
by AudioGO Ltd
by arrangement with
Golden West Literary Agency

ISBN 978 1 408 46312 3

British Library Cataloguing in Publication Data available.

Printed and bound in Great Britain by
CPI Antony Rowe, Chippenham and Eastbourne

For Joanie

The law was something to be manipulated for profit and power. The streets were dark with something more than night.

—TROUBLE IS MY BUSINESS
Raymond Chandler

— 1 —

JOE MINELLI WANTED TO STAND ON THE WAGON SEAT AND howl out his combined anger and sorrow that his talent was neglected, his keen eye and swift chisel wasted in this never-ending land of lamenting wind and lonely spaces.

A sculptor of marble statues in the old country, now he was only a disappointed stonemason driving a wagon across an enormous flat land covered with grass.

His only hope was that with this hurry-up job he'd make enough to go on to San Francisco, where he could do what he was supposed to do.

He'd been laying bricks for a barracks in Fort Riley when the quartermaster all of a sudden offered him a bonus to go out and build a monument for the first anniversary of the Battle of Wild River.

He'd ground the slaked lime and clay together for his cement, loaded the wagon with tools, and—along with his young nephew, who was crazy to be a Wild West cowboy—joined the rest of the hodgepodge wagon train.

Not a tall man, Minelli had broad shoulders and long arms overdeveloped from working with rock, and his large hands were callused from handling mortar and stone. He stared at his lime-burned fingers and shook his head bitterly, even as he wondered where that damn fool Johnny had run off to. It would have been better to leave him behind because of his foolish skylarking ways, but the kid had begged with tears in his eyes, and there was need of a boy to help mix the mortar and carry the hod. It was not correct for a maestro to do the dull physical work when one had a young apprentice to do it for him.

Yet the kid wouldn't behave like an apprentice, always running off to look at a badger den or a buffalo skeleton or a prairie dog town. By rights the boy ought to be driving the team while the maestro napped in the back of the wagon.

Basta! The sun is already in the west, he noted. Where the hell are you, Johnny?

As the trail meandered across a dried-out slough lined with big cottonwoods, Minelli lost sight of the big daugherty army ambulance ahead and another one in the lead. Even the accompanying mounted troopers were strung out, and the wagon with the burial detail lagged far behind. Even with the general

2

himself in the lead, there still was no organized formation, just because the prairie was so vast and inhuman.

While his uncle's temper smoldered, young Johnny Minelli raced the pinto pony against his own shadow, scattering rabbits and prairie chickens from their grassy haunts and crying out his own wonder of the new world.

To be free of his melancholy uncle's gloom was welcome enough, but to ride the great prairie like a cowboy or an Indian brought an unnameable ecstasy to his thirteen-year-old spirit.

Coming to a small, nearly dry creek lined with walnut trees, the pony slowed of his own accord, expecting his young rider to guide him across.

Abruptly Johnny Minelli pulled back the reins and said quickly, "Whoa!"

The pony stopped on the creek bank, hung his head, and breathed deeply, air rattling through his flared nostrils as Johnny studied a dark form almost hidden in the tree limbs. It didn't move, growl, or show its eyes.

Easing the pinto forward a slow step at a time, he saw that it was a bundle covered by a buffalo robe lashed to a scaffold of tree limbs higher than he could reach.

Working the pony close to the tree trunk, he found a low branch for a handhold and, slipping from the saddle, climbed on up.

The dusty buffalo robe was intact, and the buckskin

bindings had not broken with age. If he'd thought about it, he'd have guessed it had been there about a year.

Curiosity overcoming fear, he fetched out his jack-knife, cut the weathered lashings, and pulled aside the robe.

An integument of blackened dry skin clung to the bones. The gray hair was very long. He bit his lip as the empty eye sockets stared up at him. The lower jaw with its worn teeth had shifted to make a grotesque grin.

A breastplate of otter bones, red beads, and silver ornaments slid off the sternum, revealing a large, tarnished medallion embossed with a bearded man's profile attached to a thin chain that ran around the neck bones. Neatly folded into a parcel between the bony feet lay a warbonnet of eagle feathers trimmed with red flannel. Along the side rested a battle axe with a wide curved iron head, its long handle wrapped in buckskin and decorated with feathers.

In the back of Johnny's mind was the knowledge that the sun was in the west, that he'd been gone a long time, and that his uncle would take a leather strap to him unless he had something to show for his extended absence.

He tossed the warbonnet, the battle axe, the breast-plate, and the medallion to the ground, then shinnied down the tree after them.

Gingerly he slipped the chain of the medallion over his head, followed by the breastplate. The fancy

4

warbonnet fitted loosely on his head. With the battle axe in his left hand he mounted the patient pinto.

Looking up at the scaffold, he wished he might take the buffalo robe, too, but he'd seen how the mummified skeleton was glued to the robe by the dried fluids, and he thought it better not to push his luck any further.

As he rode out into the open again his heart thrilled with the vast unknown stretched out before him. He was a mighty Indian chief surveying his homeland. He was tall and terrible to his enemies, but venerated and respected in his teepee, where the young warriors asked for advice and squaws waited on him hand and foot.

Racing back toward the distant caravan, he watched his shadow with admiration, exulting in the power of the bonneted and armed horseman shadowed on his left side.

To his right the sun touched the flat horizon like a burning vermillion disk.

He hoped his uncle would let him keep his treasures. After all, it was finders keepers, and he'd braved the dark spirits to take them away.

As he galloped closer he noted the wagons and outriders were scattered, but all were going in the same general direction toward the site of the monument he and his uncle would build.

"I am Chief Mad Bull!" he growled at his shadow. "All men fear me!"

"Take that!" he cried out, whacking at his fearsome shadow with the battle axe. "And that!"

"Now you will behave!" he yipped in what he thought was Indian to his fallen enemy.

At that moment all thought, all memory, all meaning, and all the future disappeared for him as if a bubble had popped and he was no longer anything anywhere.

He did not see the smoke nor hear the rifle report that came from the east, nor feel the bullet smash through his face.

What was left of Johnny Minelli trembled, kicked spasmodically free of the saddle, and dropped like a falling sparrow to the ancient, ever-mothering prairie.

— 2 —

SKOFER HAAVIK, MY ANTIQUATED, BIRD-LEGGED PARTner, and I rode toward the front of the column where the general had stopped his ambulance. It still bore the standard green Maltese cross on the side, but the benches for the wounded had been pulled out and replaced by a bunk with a feather bed, as well as an easy chair, washstand, and kitchen table with two ladderback chairs. A thick black buffalo robe covered the oak planks of the wagon bed. All it needed was white lace curtains to make it home sweet home.

The canvas sides of the ambulance were rolled up, and the general gazed out from his easy chair like a Roman emperor while the bitter-faced driver waited.

"Who was shooting?" I asked.

"Have a look." The general shrugged his fat padded

7

shoulders and spit the leg bone of a grouse off into the dirt. It looked to me like General Frederick Falls hadn't missed a meal in his long army career that began in the war with Mexico. He'd no doubt been an oversized youngster with a big appetite in those days, and he'd eaten his way through the Civil War while holding down a desk job in Washington and never suffered a defeat at the table, even when he was sent out to Kansas to exterminate the Indians.

The back of his neck bulged with tallow while the front was draped with fat, pendulous wattles starting at his ears. His belly was a barrel-shaped sling for his guts, and I thought if he was a pig, he'd win the blue ribbon at the county fair.

Even his eyes, set close to his broad, upthrust nose, reminded me of a boar hog, hooded, and menacing as poisoned wells.

"Over yonder," Skofer pointed, and I saw riders approaching a figure sprawled on the prairie off to the west.

My steeldust gladly galloped across the couple hundred yards to the two men sitting in their saddles in a manner that said neither one of them cared to dismount.

The boy lay on his back, his left leg twisted underneath him at a grotesque angle. His sightless eyes stared up at the dusky sky, and a nearly bloodless bullet hole blemished his left cheek, indicating the back of the skull would be blown out.

A prime eagle-feather warbonnet lay nearby, and on his thin chest hung a fine Kiowa breastplate along with an old brass peace medallion stamped out by the great white father for his redskin children. An ominous-looking curved-headed battle axe lay close to a small flung-out hand.

"Johnny," Skofer murmured.

I nodded and noticed the rest of the wagons had turned our way.

"Damn fool," Curt Sickle, the rider closest to me, muttered dryly.

Lean and limber as a greyhound, Sickle dressed like a common cowhand in denim pants, flannel shirt, and cowhide vest. The ironshod stock of a saddle gun projected from under his right knee, and two holstered Colt .44s were tied down to either thigh as if he was afraid he might miss out on a killing. His sunburned face was nearly hairless, and his eyes reminded me of Chinese money, the brass kind with holes punched through the centers.

I knew him from down in Texas because it's my business to know gents like him.

"*Ni modo,*" the muddy-faced halfbreed opposite Sickle shrugged. An army scout, he went by the name of Snow. He wore new buckskins, and his straight black hair was half hidden by a faded denim cap he'd made from the leg of a pair of discarded jeans. Sometimes he spoke in border Spanish, sometimes in broken English, and sometimes sign language.

" 'No solution' is right," I told him, "but I'm some curious as to who'd do it."

Snow waved his hand at the converging wagons and said, "Somebody figured him for an Injun."

"I could've." Sickle grinned, challenging me.

"No." I shook my head. "You wouldn't shoot anybody for free."

His already sunburned features flushed. "In your case, don't be too sure, Mr. Benbow."

"I'll watch my back, then," I said carefully.

The boy was such a happy-go-lucky kid, skylarking all the time, it'd pleased me to watch his innocent antics. Now . . . *Ni modo,* it can't be helped.

I saw the buckboard approaching and moved the steeldust over to cut off the team.

"What is it?" Miss Sarah Duffy asked from the buckboard seat.

"The boy. Johnny's been shot."

"Dead?" She stared at me.

"Yes'm," I said. "You don't want to look."

"Mr. Benbow," she said, her wide-spaced eyes cutting with razor-sharp anger, "I'm not a ghoulish person, whatever else you might think."

"I overspoke," I said, and touched the brim of my hat.

She slapped the reins, heading the team toward the general's ambulance, which hadn't moved.

Sickle rode alongside her, and after a moment Snow, the halfbreed, followed along.

The second big daugherty pulled up nearby, and from the near-side door emerged the general's journalist, Gerald J. Barr, who went under the title of army historian. A tall, well-built man, he had shoulders that tended to bow over like he was carrying a solid lead globe of the world on his back. A trim golden mustache hardly showed on his pale face. With his head and shoulders always bowed over, it wasn't easy to see into his eyes, but what I saw was sympathetic concern and not much else.

After him came Dr. Martin Cadwell, neatly dressed in army blue, fashionably tailored to show his lean, erect build. He carried the regulation bag that held the tools of his trade. His round face was clean shaven except for fluffy reddish-gold sideburns that made his face as wide as a punkin pie surrounded by long, wavy hair.

Stepping quickly toward the body, he knelt by the dead boy without touching his knees to the grass, shook his head silently, and stood up again before the last man in the coach had descended from the iron step.

Like the other two, he was from a different world, but I'd seen enough jovial, cigar-chewing, well-upholstered politicians to know August Hamilton Root for what he was.

Never elected to public office, still he'd wriggled and elbowed and traded kumshaw all the way from a runaway kid to Assistant Secretary of War, an important man if you were in the army or navy. He could have you hanged or promoted depending on how it affected the Republican Party.

A rumor had been going around that General Falls was due to be cashiered for botching the Battle of Wild River or given another star for the historic victory, depending on the party's political plans.

August Hamilton Root didn't go near the body.

Instead he stepped around to the rear of the daugherty, opened his arms wide as he viewed the sun slowly setting over the flat western horizon, and declaimed:

> "Take them, O great Eternity!
> Our little life is but a gust
> That bends the branches of thy tree,
> And trails its blossoms in the dust. . . ."

as if he'd just made up Longfellow's lines.

Root's chubby features were sharpened by a long, slanted mustache and a sharp-pointed goatee that made me see him two ways: the jolly politico and the conniving, mean skunk he probably was. Maybe it takes two faces to get up that high, or, as Skofer said, "down that low."

Without even acknowledging our presence, the three gents climbed back into the daugherty and followed Sarah Duffy toward the general's private ambulance.

A minute later the broad-wheeled wagon driven by Joe Minelli pulled up. I backed off the steeldust as the heavy-shouldered mason leapt down from the seat and ran to the boy's side.

Touching the pallid face, he looked up and stared at us.

"Who did this?" he cried out in shocked horror.

"No one's said yet," Skofer murmured sympathetically.

12

"It's murder!" His voice turned deep and harsh. "Somebody goin' die for it!"

"Maybe it was an accident, Joe," I said. "Let me ask around before you pay off the wrong man."

"If it takes me the rest of my life," he yelled, "I'm goin' to cut his heart out!"

Slight and slender, the general's son, Lieutenant Billy Falls, rode up on a handsome gray gelding and dismounted. "I'm very sorry, Mr. Minelli," he said.

"You do this?" Minelli stared at him fiercely, his big hands working.

"No, sir," the lieutenant said, looking over the top of Minelli's head. "The general wishes me to bring the trophies to him."

"Trophies!" Minelli groaned and looked down at the dead boy. "I'm goin' get a trophy back, you bet!"

Lieutenant Falls carefully slipped the brass medal and the breastplate loose, picked up the feathered bonnet and the battle axe, and mounted up again.

"We'll meet in camp," he said crisply, and he kicked the gray into an easy gallop back toward the gathering wagons and troopers.

Dragging up the rear came the burial detail, soldiers so worthless they hadn't enough gumption to desert and go on west as half of the Western Division troopers had already done.

Four of them rode in a big wide-wheeled lumber wagon stacked with picks and shovels and wooden crosses.

They paused, and the sergeant who had the reins

spit ambeer over the wheel, looked at the crumpled form, and shook his head.

"He's not ours." He slapped the reins on the mules' butts.

"You devil," Joe Minelli yelled, running at the placid sergeant. "Give me a cross at least!"

"You don't get no cross usin' language like that," the sergeant growled. "Tell it to the general."

The wagon passed on by, and I said, "Wrap him in a blanket, Joe. We can bury him in the army cemetery tomorrow."

"No! No!" He backed away from me like he was afraid I'd use force on him. "He stays where he falls. I dig. I make him monument, too."

"Can we help?" Skofer asked.

"Help!" he cried out bitterly. "Yes, you give me the man!"

We left him in the gathering dusk, cutting out the tight sod. Beneath, it would be easy digging.

The wagons had been drawn up in a loose circle and the animals hobbled and left out on the range without a guard because there were no more Kiowas left to run them off.

The general had made sure of that.

Not quite so confident, I picketed my steeldust close to my bedroll.

"You don't want to get a little closer to camp?" Skofer asked.

"It's not our camp," I said. "We didn't ask for an invite, and they didn't offer."

14

As far as I was concerned, I wished we hadn't even seen the general and his entourage.

Our job was to find a crazy nester named Mordecai Jones, who thought he could take over the river crossing that had been used by cattle drivers up from Texas since they started.

The commander had told me to fix it so that members of the South Texas Cattlemen's Association had nothing to complain about.

"I'm just a brand inspector," I'd protested mildly.

"Now you're a river crossing inspector." The commander'd given me his regulation fat smile that told me nothing, and I'd headed for the door when he called after me, "Take Skofer along with you. He'll drink himself to death hanging around here."

We'd come around through Ellsworth—that was the last stop for the Kansas Pacific—asked some of the drovers about the river crossing, and got the same story every time.

—Yes indeedy, there was a crazy homesteader had filed on the crossing even though there were better claims up or down the river. He spent most of his time chasing away any prospective neighbors and trying to build a fence but hadn't had much luck with it because the herds pushed right through the rails. Made him mad, all right. Waved a shotgun around, but nobody'd called him on it yet. . . .

That "yet" was too ominous. We didn't need a reputation for murdering sodbusters, no matter how much we hated the sonsabitches. We were pushing for

15

a national cattle trail from Texas to Montana, and it wouldn't help at all if a trigger-happy cowboy happened to pot the poor family man defending his home, so to speak.

The crossing was supposed to be near the site of the general's massacre of the Kiowas the year before, and we'd had the luck—good or bad I wasn't sure—to head down the trail at the same time the general's advance detail started off to bury the remains left behind, clean up the site, and dedicate the historical spot as a National Cemetery and Preserve.

While Skofer roasted sliced sow belly over our small fire I dug out the day-old corn pone that was going to be our supper.

"Poor little tyker," Skofer muttered.

"Whoever did it better own up to it," I said.

"Probably an accident."

"Near perfect shooting." I shook my head.

"It wasn't the burial detail," Skofer said, "and likely not Miss Sarah Duffy."

"That cuts it down to Company B and about eight others, then," I said, putting a crackly piece of bacon between a couple slices of corn pone and taking a bite.

"Maybe we better just stick to business," Skofe said. "I wonder if those folks happened to bring a keg of liquor along."

"The commander seemed to think you were already well saturated."

"So that's the game!" Skofer jumped to his feet and stuck out his bony chest like a banty rooster. "Now you're saying I need a nursemaid, and you know damn well I been bone dry since we left Ellsworth!"

"'Course, Ellsworth was flood time." I nodded agreeably.

I didn't want to remind him that I'd found him in the corner of Luther Knoby's Horseshoe Saloon being trampled by a crowd of cowboys who figured they were walking on horse biscuits.

"I could say some things," he said huffily. "I could tell some stories, mister, about a certain wet horse blanket that couldn't laugh for fear it'd crack his face!"

"I reckon." I smiled in the dark, because it's always a pleasure to hear his inventions.

"By damn! I've a mind to just split the blanket and go back to Ellsworth," he jabbered on.

"And miss the big ceremony?" I teased him.

"Glad to," he snapped. "It's nothing but cool blue smoke to feed the newspapers back east."

"I heard Senator McReynolds and General Phil Sheridan were coming. Maybe even General Sherman . . ."

"I wouldn't mind taking a shot at him," Skofer muttered. "Maybe I'll stay and think on that."

"And that brings us around to who bushwhacked the kid," I said, getting to my feet. "You want to mosey over to the big he-boar's camp?"

We kept on talking so they'd know we were coming, even though we weren't making much sense.

"Evenin'," I said, entering the firelight where the

general's people sat around the dying blaze. The burial detail, being all enlisted men, were camped on downwind with Company B.

General Falls's bulk filled a canvas and oak camp chair. The others sat on crates and upended buckets so they all seemed like dwarfs at the court of the corpulent king.

Two people didn't fit in with the general's underlings. One was the young lady, Sarah Duffy, and the other was the hired killer, Curt Sickle.

I knew Sarah Duffy intended to look for her brother's remains, but Curt Sickle's being there made no sense at all unless he'd been hired to kill someone in the group. His story that he was just sightseeing made as much sense as a buzzard chasing butterflies.

The man was a known bounty hunter, usually legal. Anyone who knew different wasn't talking about it.

I hunkered down on my heels and chewed on a straw, waiting like the rest for the general to speak.

"These trophies are evidence of Chief Wide Bear's death last year at Wild River. Be sure you get every detail in your story, Barr."

"Yes, sir." The tall, pallid man nodded.

"I knew I'd killed him, but he was dragged off in the heat of battle before I could take his scalp," the general said. "Got that?"

"Yes, sir," Barr said, making notes on a pad of paper.

"Fill in the details on how he sneaked up behind me with his axe—"

18

"Then you threw him over your head and shot him with your Henry carbine?" Barr murmured.

"That'll do to start with," the general said. "Flesh it out, though. Bigger than life. Don't hold anything back."

"Yes, sir." Barr nodded.

"Talkin' about carbines, what about the kid?" I put in mildly.

"Are you speaking of the young hod carrier?" The general squeezed his full lips together like he was going to spit on me.

"I'm wondering who killed him," I said, "and why."

"Obviously someone thought he was an attacking Indian," the general said flatly, looking around.

"That's right," Root agreed quickly. The others nodded like they had hinges in their necks.

"Then why doesn't somebody just come out and admit it?" I held on, trying to keep the anger out of my voice.

"What concern is it of yours?" young Lieutenant Falls asked quickly.

"The kid was a human being, and thanks to the general, we all know there are no Indians left around here," I said.

"But everyone has a carbine," the lieutenant said.

"It was an accident," Root spoke up. "Someone made a quick shot before he had time to think."

"A head shot at two hundred yards or more?"

I let the question hang there until Sarah Duffy said,

19

"No one wishes the boy's uncle to have the wrong idea."

"Especially when he's the only one that can build the monument," I said with a nod.

"It could have been anybody," Dr. Cadwell said. "Best let it lie."

"Seems like it pretty much had to come from someone sitting right here," I said mildly.

"That's enough," the general growled, squeezing his fat lips together again. "It is none of your affair. Drop the matter at once."

"I was thinkin' that Joe Minelli's mad enough to kill us all just to be sure of gettin' the one that did it," I said, ignoring the general's brusque command.

"The Italians are that way," Skofer added.

"If someone would just explain it to him, maybe he'd understand and forget about revenge." I looked around at each face. There was Sickle next to Sarah, Duffy, Barr, and Doc Cadwell, Lieutenant Falls, Root, and the general, all staring into the fire, pretending they didn't hear me. Snow sat off by himself.

"I'll have him put in irons," the general rumbled.

"You've got to have that monument on time, general," I said. "Better get the truth out and clear the air."

"From your lazy hookworm drawl, I take it you were a traitor to the Union," the general growled.

"I wouldn't call it that, General," I said. "If we'd won, I doubt if we'd have taken such cruel revenge on you folks."

"Steady, Sam," Skofer murmured.

"You're insolent," the general said harshly. "I'll not

tolerate it. Billy, bring out the plaque and read it to this ignorant turncoat."

"Yessir." The lieutenant hurried around to the side of the general's private ambulance and a moment later returned with a heavy bronze tablet covered with cast lettering.

"All of it?" the young officer asked hesitantly.

"Did I not say 'read it'?" The general's voice was loaded with scorn and contempt.

"Yessir." The lieutenant turned so that the fire lighted the plaque, and he read slowly, "Near this spot, on the fifth day of September, 1869, Brigadier General Frederick Falls, with the Second, Third, and Fourth Cavalry regiments, although greatly outnumbered, courageously defeated the savage Kiowa hordes with minimal losses and cleared the plains for peaceful settlement.

"To honor the Victory of Wild River, this hallowed place shall be henceforth known as General Frederick Falls Cemetery and Land Preserve. How sleep the brave. Signed, Ulysses S. Grant, President."

I saw a tear roll down Sarah Duffy's rounded cheek in the silence that followed.

"Jesus," I said, getting to my feet and backing off a step, "who wrote that garbage?"

"How dare you, sir?" Gerald Barr reared back and faced me. "I wrote those words, and I'll not have them insulted by a common saddle tramp."

"Southern rebel hookworm trash," the general added. "Put the plaque back, Lieutenant."

"My brother may have been on that battlefield,"

Sarah Duffy said sharply. "You have no right to question his courage."

"I reckon it'll all come out someday, ma'am," I said. "I'm sorry about your brother."

"That river used to be called Putrid Creek," Snow said seriously from the edge of the firelight. "It never was called Wild River because it ain't never been wild."

"But Wild River sounds better, doesn't it?" Gerald Barr said patiently. "The general likes Wild River."

"Sure, but it ain't right." The halfbreed still didn't understand why they'd change the name.

"I picked the name, Snow," General Falls said. "By now it's world famous, and it is right."

"*'Sta bien,*" Snow said slowly, fading back into the shadows.

"We're not gettin' the boy's killin' aired out," I said quietly. "I'm just askin' for someone to explain it."

"We are finished with the discussion." The general smiled like a bulldog eating a doughnut. "Even a nincompoop like Dr. Cadwell knows when to quit, right, Doctor?"

"Whatever you say, sir." Cadwell flushed red in the glow of the fire's coals, his left hand drifting over his wavy hair.

The general was enjoying himself.

"You don't think it was deliberate?" Sarah Duffy frowned, her large dark eyes fixed on me like I was a skunk at a church picnic.

"If no one speaks up, then it's cold-blooded murder, and you can all try to live with it," I said.

"That's enough!" the general roared from deep in the middle of his paunch. "You have no authority here, no reason to be here. Get out!"

"You don't care about simple justice?" I asked.

"The only thing that concerns me now is that my monument is built on time!" he snarled.

— 3 —

BEFORE DAYBREAK THE CHILL CAME UP OUT OF THE earth like an icy magnet drawn to the little cannonball splinter buried in my hip. I tried the other side, but it was too late. The ache wouldn't go away, and I couldn't lie there listening to the coyotes' howls in the distance and Skofer's blissful rasp and gurgle, broken occasionally by a snort and a smothered giggle. Whoever or whatever he was waltzing in his dream sure must've been a tickly little piece of calico.

Silently cussing the artillery man whose work had awakened me and who was probably dead by now, I slipped on my boots, put on my hat, carried my all-purpose blanket and pillow over to the steeldust, and settled them over his back.

The pale yellow moon was setting like a brass

24

button on a blue coat, and the prairie was lighted by a milky haze cast down by the stars.

The boy's violent death was still on my mind because the general and his bootlickers meant to pretend that it didn't even happen, or if it did, that he was just a fool kid, and that's life.

Somehow they forgot that we'd all been fool kids once, and nobody had killed us for it.

I'd only seen the boy a couple of times, waved hello, glimpsed his wide eyes and big smile, and wished I had some of that fresh time left in me.

Maybe I saw something of myself in him, something I liked to remember—that gushing wonder and joy in exploring each new day.

Forget it, I told myself. He's deader'n a china doorknob, and it's none of your business. Maybe Sarah Duffy doesn't know who did it, but the rest of them in that camp do. Let them pay whatever price conscience costs when the ghost of that boy rides through their dreams.

I have a strange belief that if you do a rotten thing or share in it, you pay in the still times. Say you're loafing by a pretty running stream watching big rainbow trout jumping for the twilight's hatch, and just when you think you're in tune with the whole beautiful world the skeleton of a boy wearing a warbonnet rides right through the middle of it.

To me, that's hard pay.

A pink flush on the eastern flats reminded me dawn was not far behind, and I singlefooted the steeldust off toward a faint amber light that looked out of place against a sky of glittering stars.

The lantern outlined the mason's wagon, and approaching slowly, I saw Joe Minelli bending over a slab of limestone with a chisel in one hand and a mallet in the other.

He heard me coming and stared into the misty star glow.

"It's only me, Sam Benbow," I called softly, hoping not to awaken the army camp only a couple hundred yards away.

"Come on," he said, and he went back to work.

I walked the steeldust into the lantern light and stepped down.

"Up early," I said.

"I don't sleep," he muttered, tapping away.

I looked over his shoulder and saw the sharp-cut lettering: GIOVANNI MINELLI. Beneath that was carved AGED 13, and under that, MURDERED.

"Nice work," I said, "and a nice stone, too."

"I brought this stone for their damn monument," he growled, "but it's too good for them."

He ran his big, hard hands over the face of the stone gently, as if he were touching the face of the boy; then, squatting on bent knees, he grabbed hold, lifted it to his chest, walked a few yards to the edge of the lantern light, and placed the stone flat on the mound of earth.

"I don't want it stickin' up," he muttered, like he was talking to himself. "In a year it would fall down. This way it stays where it belongs."

He took off his floppy woolen hat and looked at me. "You know a prayer?"

"No," I said, "but he doesn't need one."

"Good-bye, Johnny," he said. "Don't worry, they'll pay back double."

"Joe," I said quickly, "you can't win against these people. Let me try to work it out."

"Why you? You ain't a Minelli," he growled.

"Because you're a master stonemason, and I'm more of a master of murder."

"I think it was the general or his kid," Joe said bitterly.

"Did you see them?"

"No. I was way behind, but they were close enough."

"So were the others."

"You better be quick," he muttered, blowing out the lantern.

A pale lavender light flooded over the great pasture, and clouds in the east were rouged underneath by the down-under sun. From the wagons men were groaning as they came awake to face the new day.

Riding back to our little camp, I wasn't sure if Minelli would hold off his vengeance or not. Like most solitary men brought up to think in a different language, he lived in his own secluded inner jungle where the black panther's muscles ripple and its golden eyes shine in the darkness.

Skofer had a buffalo-chip fire going, the coffeepot on, and the bacon roasting on green sticks. With his rumpled gray wispy hair and gray stubble on his thin, lined features, he looked older than Methuselah's grandfather, but his faded blue eyes were chipper and clear.

"Just in time." He smiled, showing his worn-down teeth. "I was fixing to eat your half first."

"Have a good night?" I asked, ground-tying the steeldust and hunkering down by the fire.

"Couldn't sleep a wink." He shook his head dolefully. "I just stared at the stars and remembered all the debts I haven't paid."

"And never will." I nodded, pouring a cup of coffee.

"If you'd quit spending all our money on down-and-out widder women and orphans and such, I reckon I could!" he fired back at me. "We could have made it out to San Juan Bautista again and got you married off to Doña Encarnacion, taken over her ranch and lived like California dons the rest of our blessed days."

"We're too late, Skofe," I said, digging out a folded piece of paper from my breast pocket.

He gave me a suspicious look as he unfolded the letter and read out loud, "Dearest Sam, *mi vida, mi alma, mi corazón*. Why you break my heart so much? Why don't you come to my side and guard the Sanchez treasure? I have waited and waited for you, and now I must marry another. *Te quiero mucho. Adios amor. Chona* (Doña Encarnacion Sanchez).

"Maybe it's not too late," he said thoughtfully.

It was his favorite subject ever since we had ridden through the little mission village and were invited to stay at Doña Encarnacion's hacienda. She'd had four husbands die on her, and the pretty little thing wasn't even twenty years old yet. Her ranch covered fifty square miles of the richest range a cowman would ever want to ride. She wouldn't stop crying until I had promised we'd be back. That was a couple years ago, and still on my mind. I just didn't want to talk about it before I had my coffee.

"I won't go poor with my hat in my hand."

"You promised her." He kept at it.

"Soon as we make a stake," I said, "likely we'll be there for Christmas, and she'll be widowed again."

"Likely." He nodded solemnly.

We finished up the simple breakfast, packed the horses, and were ready to move out when the sun lifted like a pot of molten gold in the east and the first breeze of the day wafted through, presaging the daily prairie wind that was just fine on a hot day but would drive lonely folks crazy if they ever stopped to listen to its sad lament.

As we rode toward the soldiers' camp I saw Miss Sarah Duffy tying a striped cotton shawl over her reddish brown hair and lithely climbing into her buckboard in a way that would have been called unladylike anywhere else.

As we approached the general's special ambulance I heard him giving the day's order to Snow.

"Go ahead and keep a lookout, but find us some antelope or deer, too. I want meat."

"Yessir." The halfbreed nodded and touched the stock of his saddle gun. "I can do that."

"Forward!" the general yelled at the lieutenant up on his gray gelding.

"HO!" The lieutenant yelled, waving his arm forward.

The others followed at irregular distances, with the burial detail wagon bringing up the rear as always.

The trail was marked by other wagon wheels that had passed along this way in other times. Not heavily traveled, it was the north and south route between central Kansas and the Nations and would cross the river somewhere below the battleground, right about where the crazy nester named Mordecai Jones thought he had more rights than other homesteaders or Texas cattlemen.

Off to the east I pointed out a dusty smudge and said, "Let's have a look."

"Guess it won't hurt," Skofer said, still feisty, but as I put the steeldust into a slow canter straight into the morning sun he chuckled like a billy goat in clover and started screeching:

> "O Susan Van Dusan,
> The girl of my choosin'
> The size of your bosom
> Would make a man moo-oo-oo—"

I guessed that was a sign he was over the hardest part of the dry season.

The stretched-out herd looked to be a little more than two thousand critters road-branded with a simple H. We stayed clear in case they were a spooky bunch set to stampede and rode parallel for a while until a point rider turned our way.

We pulled up as he approached, and I recognized Hack Berry from over in Uvalde County, a member of the association.

"Howdy," he said, pulling up his heavy-shouldered claybank. "Benbow, ain't it? Skofer. What you boys doin' so far away from home?"

His thin, bony face was burned to the color of desert mahogany, and it made his blue eyes look like shining ice.

"You're makin' good time, Hack," I commented.

"Lost a day back at the river," he said, eyeing me, knowing what I wanted. "Crazy man and a bunch of his kin tryin' to put a fence up."

"Gunplay?" I asked, because he wasn't saying any more.

"No," he said tightly. "I give him fair warning, but he wanted to charge me by the head to pass through. Somehow me'n a couple of the boys got the drop on him whilst the others pulled down his damn fence and pushed the herd across."

"He show fight?"

"Oh, my, yes, he's just a low-heeled fightin' fool. Was worse after we roped him." Hack let a smile ripple over his bronzed face.

"I'm supposed to try to move him someplace else."

"That's your job, I reckon," he said, looking back at the herd. "But he's so stubborn I doubt he'd move camp for a prairie fire."

"Thanks, Hack," I said as he kneed the claybank back to the herd.

We turned southwest, aiming to join the wagon train before it reached the turnoff to the battle ground.

"Old Hack's slowin' down," Skofer said. "Why didn't he just shoot the damn nester and pass on by?"

"Guess he figured that was our job."

"We aren't goin' to shoot him, are we?" he asked, staring at me.

"What's the matter, you slowin' down some?" I grinned.

"You know I never shoot anybody unless it's strictly in self-defense. I don't have no trouble sleeping at night." He started jabbering again. "You're the one to watch. Kill crazy. Mad dog. I thought last night you were trying to provoke a bloodbath that'd keep that burial detail busy for a week."

"Me? Jolly old raisin puddin' pie Benbow? Hell, I'm yellow as mustard without the bite!"

The wagon train had made the turnoff for upriver, and we took off after them, going along at an easy lope that put us even with them by the time the sun was overhead.

From his easy chair the general shouted at his son, the lieutenant, to turn this way, then that way.

"Lieutenant, I seriously doubt if you could find your pecker with your hand!" the general roared sarcastically.

Of course, the lieutenant had never been there before, and the general wouldn't help.

The journalist, Barr, was the only other one in the

party who knew the battlefield, but he was back in his daugherty composing more fiction, likely.

Skofer and I rode ahead to a rise above the old flood plain where we could see the big bend in the river that had been the traditional summer camp of the Kiowa.

The story as I'd heard it in the Brindle Bull Saloon in Austin from a tired old trooper who'd deserted after the battle was that after the cavalry camped about five miles upriver, the general sent his staff officers down to Wide Bear with a bunch of presents and told him that he'd like to come visit the next afternoon. The officers reported back that there were less than three hundred warriors in the camp, about the same number of women and children, and maybe a thousand horses.

The general then made a surprise attack at day-break, catching the Kiowas in bed—a "brilliant maneuver"—and as the river was on the rise his forces slaughtered and burned the whole camp in a matter of minutes. Only two things went wrong. He sent a company after a few braves fleeing downriver and didn't know there was a second village just around the bend. That detachment ran into warriors that were warned and ready. The troopers disap-peared. The general, not knowing why, ordered a retreat, but the Indians' horse herd slowed them down, and the general ordered the entire herd shot.

The trooper, half drunk and hollow-eyed, said it took them an hour to kill all those horses. It hurt him worse than killing the women and children because those were real fine ponies.

"What about the lost company?"

"They must be dead. We'll never know, because the general wouldn't let anyone go around the bend to find out."

"Don't hardly seem right leaving your dead and wounded behind," I'd said.

"We run the other way. But Lord God—all those fine ponies . . ."

It was all there to see from the rise.

The general's ambulance pulled up close by, and I heard him bellow, "Stop the team, you damned idiot, this is it!"

"Yessir," the driver said, setting the brake as the general hoisted himself out of the chair and lumbered toward the side door.

By the time he'd managed to clamber to the ground the rest of the train arrived.

Skofe and I dismounted and ground-tied our horses off to the side of the rise.

The general, huffing and puffing from the exertion needed to get out of the ambulance, waited until everyone, including the burial detail, was assembled.

"There it is, gentlemen!" Falls waved a swollen hand at the flat ground below. "You can see it all from here.

"We came from the northwest. The second regiment next to the river, the third to its left, and the fourth on the left flank.

"The strategy was to drive the enemy before us with their backs to the river. This was carried out with perfect precision, and the battle was won before breakfast."

I looked across at the flat land nestled in the arm of the river and saw heaps of half-burned buffalo robes, charred lodge poles, and scattered bones.

"It must have been inspirational to see the whole thing happen right before your eyes," August Hamilton Root said.

"Of course, if that old wound from Chickamauga hadn't prevented me, I'd have been at the head of the attack," Falls said, eyeing Gerald Barr, who was sketching the scene on a heavy piece of paper with pen and ink.

"I'll make a note of it, General," Barr said without looking up.

"Is it true that the Kiowas were flying an American flag you'd given them the day before—and a white flag of truce, too?" I asked mildly.

"That is an absolute lie!" the general roared, and he turned on me. "If you dare open your mouth again, I'll see that it's the last time!"

"An awful lot of bones." Doc Cadwell sniffed, stroking his wavy hair. "You'd think they'd at least bury their dead."

Off to the right the land curved up and made a gentle little basin that should have been deep in grass, but it looked more like a blizzard had hit it. The bones of the slaughtered horse herd were so thick the brown grass was mostly hidden. God, how the wolves must have feasted all winter!

"Indeed"—the general had a coughing spell—"we might find half a dozen of our missing troopers in that mess, men who at the time we believed had been killed in action and their mutilated bodies thrown into the river by the enemy."

"And where would the men of Company A of the Fourth Regiment be?" Sarah Duffy asked quietly.

"Downriver no more than a mile around the bend. They were ambushed and driven into the river. We found no trace of them."

"You did look?" she asked firmly, her wide-spaced dark eyes fixed on the general as the prairie wind teased a wisp of reddish brown hair across her forehead.

"Of course we looked!" the general growled. "Ask Gerald Barr. He was here by my side."

Showing his irritation at meddlesome women, Gerald Barr took his attention away from the sketch, put the small pen and ink bottle in their silver-bound pocket case, and turned toward Sarah very deliberately.

I noted some pink coloration on each cheekbone, as if he'd been using rouge, or was madder than he let on.

"Miss Duffy, the battle was conducted exactly as the general has explained. We believe Company A was ambushed, and that the cowardly savages fled afterward."

"I will look," she said simply, turning away.

"Bring the sergeant and the stonemason at once, Lieutenant," the general commanded, and young Falls trotted off to find them.

36

"Splendid, simply splendid." Root smiled, viewing the scene and rocking back on his heels. "You should at least have a Medal of Honor, General."

"You know what I want, Root," the general said sharply.

"I'm afraid it is out of my hands. I did make my recommendation, though."

"When will we know?"

"The courier may arrive at any time . . . or never. Who can say? You know I'm on your side," Root said warmly.

When Lieutenant Falls arrived with the beefy sergeant and Joe Minelli, the general pointed off at a frame of half-burned lodge poles near the center of the riverbend and said to Minelli, "Mark that spot. That's where you build the monument."

"I gotta find the rocks first," Minelli said slowly.

"Get at it. I'll give you two days, and if you botch the job, goddamn you, I'll hang you by your dago heels!" the general snapped.

Minelli quietly climbed aboard his wagon and headed the team toward the river.

"Sergeant!" the general yelled.

"Yes, sir!" The sergeant stepped forward, stood at attention, and saluted for good measure.

"Yes, yes," the general growled, "you take your goddamned bunch of malingerin' bounty jumpers down there and find six skeletons that look like they belong to us. You dig a deep grave behind the monument and bury those bones. You place six crosses, three wide and two deep, to indicate separate graves.

You then police the entire area and throw everything left over into the river. I want that riverbend clean as a new white glove."

"Yessir!" the sergeant responded loudly.

"One more thing, Sergeant." The general glared at me. "If these two civilians interfere in any way, I want them punished. Clear?"

"Yessir!" The sergeant glanced my way, saluted again, and marched off to gather up the burial detail.

"My brother?" Sarah Duffy asked firmly.

"My dear lady, if you or the detail find the remains of your brother, we shall of course take appropriate action," the general said as if he was charitably holding onto his temper. "Believe me, Miss Duffy, the army looks after its own."

"I do hope that is the case," she replied, giving him no quarter.

I began to see there was more to her than just a sharp-tongued spinster. She knew her duty and meant to do it.

Two of the general's orderlies got busy setting up camp, and I looked around for an out-of-the-way spot for us to spend the night.

"You want to stay a couple days and watch the show?" I asked Skofer.

"You think Sherman's coming?"

"I dunno . . . There's some other dirty business going on besides the general's circus," I said, "but I don't suppose you're interested."

"Hell, they've already kilt the Indians," Skofer

squawked as we led our horses away from the main camp. "What's left?"

"Minelli," I said.

A little fold in the side of the hill gave us some protection from the wind, and we unloaded our packs and called it home.

"We can take a *pasear* on down to the crossing later on," I said, wondering if Miss Sarah Duffy had gone out looking yet. "But let's make a little circle around the bend just for fun."

"Sam Benbow," Skofer grumbled, crawling rickety-like up into his saddle, "putting a bee up the general's butt is not my notion of fun."

We rode an arc northerly, passing by the coulee full of bleached and gnawed horse bones, which I figured was a sort of wartime lesson taught by William T. Sherman: If you can't steal it, burn it or kill it.

I'd seen enough of his work.

We went on around to the east so that when we turned south we'd come to the river downstream from the big bend, out of sight of the general and his burial detail.

We went into the trees to get a look at Putrid Creek, now called Wild River, and found it was neither a creek nor a wild river. At this time of the year it was three quarters full of slow-moving muddy water. Here the steep banks were lined with willows and cotton-woods, along with clumps of chokecherry and sandhill plums.

Bits of old driftage caught in the trees higher than

my head showed that it could be a formidable stream at flood stage.

"Was it a dry year last year?" I asked Skofer.

"Not for me it wasn't." He cackled like an old fool.

Farther on south I thought I saw the buckboard of Sarah Duffy, with Curt Sickle trailing along behind on his big black gelding.

4

WHETHER HE SAW US OR NOT I COULDN'T TELL, BUT ONE minute he was there between us and the distant buckboard, and the next minute he wasn't anywhere.

"Must've moved off into the trees," Skofer said, standing in his stirrups and blinking his eyes.

"That's where a backshooter'd go," I said.

I looked at the tracks where he'd forced the black through a clump of chokecherries into the cotton-woods, and passed on by.

"Think he bushwhacked the boy?" Skofer asked as I put the steeldust into a fast trot.

"Could've been almost anyone except his uncle and the gravediggers. They were too far behind."

"I still wonder why," Skofer grumbled as he bounced around on his saddle, not liking the gait.

41

I kneed the steeldust up a notch to a slow canter, and Skofer's roan changed leads and joined him.

"Pure meanness," I said.

"There's aplenty of that in this outfit," Skofer said, settling down to the easy rhythm.

About the time the horses started enjoying the canter we caught up with Sarah Duffy, an unmarried lady not more than twenty-five years old, and they settled down to a walk again.

"Afternoon, ma'am," I said, touching my hat. "Don't it kind of bother you driving out here alone?"

"No." She looked across at me, a trace of a smile on her heart-shaped face. "Mr. Spencer rides along."

She lifted a blanket beside her, revealing a .56-50 Indian Model Spencer carbine by her side.

"Can you use that?" I asked, trying not to look surprised.

"My brother is a good shot and a good teacher as well, Mr. Benbow," she replied.

"I hope he's in good health, too," I said carefully. "Where do you think he is?"

"We know the desertion rate of the frontier cavalry is more than fifty percent," she said, as if she'd said the speech so often in her head it was memorized. "That means there's a fifty-fifty chance he was never in this battle. He might well be in California."

"Wouldn't he write?" Skofer asked.

"Possibly he's sick or disabled in some way and cannot." She shrugged her straight-across shoulders. "I have absolute faith that he's alive."

42

"He might have been here and been taken captive, too," I said.

"That's less likely, I should think." She set her jaw firmly. "There were no captives taken on either side, except for a few girls that were saved out for the officers."

"You speak plain enough," I said, wondering what made her such a tough, unyielding rock of a person, yet with an essential feminine manner.

How much of the hardness was bluff? How much of it was just sheer nerve? I couldn't think of a single decent woman who would come out here to the middle of Kansas alone.

The only females who traveled alone were of ill repute, moving from one whorehouse to another, and Miss Sarah Duffy had none of the earmarks of a sporter. The gray cotton blouse was buttoned clear up to her throat, and underneath, her bosom must have been wrapped around and bound down tightly, because although there was a considerable bulge, there was no motion at all. She wore no sporter warpaint, and her long hair was braided and then coiled up in a bun.

"Teach school?" I asked.

"Does it show?" She smiled.

"Some."

"I'm trying to look like a warden in a nunnery," she said sheepishly.

"Keep trying," I said, "you're close."

"Actually, I was raised on a farm in Indiana, but

after my parents died, we lost it. School teaching was the only thing left for me."

We were following the riverbank's slow turns by keeping out of the timber on high ground, and we had seen no trace of battle, no rips in the earth, no spent cartridges, no rags or bones.

"No offense, Miss Duffy," I said, "but if we find this second village, it'll look pretty bad. Maybe I could save you some—"

"Grief?" she interrupted. "Shock at the horror? No, thanks. The only way I can know for sure is to see it with my own eyes."

"You saw how it was up at the main battlefield. How will you tell . . ."

"I am rather hoping he will not be here. But if he is, he'll have a front tooth made of cast tin. Also, his spurs were not regulation. I gave them to him for Christmas."

"What was special about his spurs?" Skofer asked.

She glanced over at him and, blushing, said, "They had the 'gal-leg' shank mounted with a silver stocking and a gold slipper and garter."

"Yes'm," Skofer croaked, "I've seen some like that down in Texas."

"Gal's legs?" I asked.

"Spurs!" Skofer said indignantly, then he figured I was joshing him and muttered, "You gol-darned idjit . . ."

The shadows of the trees stretched out long to the east, and I could feel the chill following the westering sun touching my shoulders.

44

"Perhaps we should start back and look tomorrow," she said. "I'm not much for traveling in the dark."

"I appreciate a sensible woman," Skofer said, making a smile. "I've known some that couldn't tell day from night."

"I suppose you've known a great many, Mr. . . ."

"Haavik," Skofer said quickly, "but just call me Skofe. Haavik sounds too much like a tornado going by, and I'm just a zephyr of a breeze."

He was jabbering, trying to get out of the hole he'd dug for himself.

"You haven't answered my question, Skofe." She looked at him sternly.

I couldn't tell whether she was laughing inside or not.

"Women? The answer is no. I'm so shy of the female gender I generally run for the nearest saloon if I hear one tiptoeing through the canebrakes."

"You're sweet," she said, nodding. "You have a certain mature dignity that younger men lack."

I thought Skofer would float right out of his saddle and blind us with the rosy sunbeams radiating off his wizened-up face.

"Thank you, ma'am. You certainly have a discerning eye," he allowed. "Too often folks notice a big, clumsy, rough-cut fellow like Sam and can't see past his bulk to the real quality."

"You speak like an educated person," she said pleasantly. "Where did you go to school?"

"I *taught* at the University of Virginia a few years

ago," Skofer said loftily. "Unfortunately, I couldn't return after the war."

"Why not?" she asked, turning the team to the left, away from the river toward higher ground.

"I was a professor of divinity," he said slowly. "After the war I couldn't teach anything I didn't believe in."

"At least you're honest about it," she said.

I looked back as we made the turn on the high ground and saw the abandoned, fallen-down lodges.

"There it is," I interrupted their mature tater-tater.

She hauled on the reins and looked over her shoulder at the distant scene.

"What do you make of it?" Skofer asked.

"A fair guess would be the company ran onto the village before they knew it, then tried to get the hell out, beggin' your pardon, ma'am."

"But what happened to the Indians?" she whispered, staring in horror.

"Likely they figured the general had 'em outnumbered and fogged out in a hurry."

"But where did they go?"

"North," I said. "They're some shirt-tail kin of the Sioux. We'll get a better look tomorrow, ma'am."

"What do you think, Skofe?" she asked.

"In this case, I yield to the wisdom of my junior colleague," Skofe pontificated grandly.

"I'll be back," she murmured to no one in particular.

* * *

She wouldn't let Skofer, who was trying to, nor me, who was not trying to, unharness her team.

"But it isn't ladylike," Skofer objected.

"There's nothing on a farm that's ladylike," she said with a chuckle. "Ergo, there are no ladies on farms, only farmers' daughters."

Before he could counter with his theories on maidenly women, Gerald Barr, tall and hump-shouldered as a sandhill crane, ambled over, smiled crookedly, and said, "Snow killed probably the last buffalo in existence this afternoon. Would you care to have supper with us?"

"All of us?" she asked sharply.

"Of course." He made a short, ironic bow. "The general's nerves always improve later in the day."

"You mean he drinks?" Skofer licked his lips.

"Moderately." Barr smiled again and raised his cocked right hand high as he could.

"It takes one to know one." Skofer nodded wisely.

"I'm just about burned out on sowbelly and corn dodgers," I said, smelling the roast buffalo on the wind. I felt like running up to the rise and whacking off a couple of pounds for my first bite.

"We'd be honored to accept." Skofer made a short bow to the tall journalist.

I'd wondered why Barr was short of breath and why the roses bloomed on his cheekbones, until he coughed politely into his fist.

The TB didn't care how old you were, how many doctors you could afford, or your race, creed, or color.

47

Once it started nibbling at your lungs, you'd best start making something out of what little life you had left.

We walked along with him, and his breath grew short and hoarse halfway up the gentle slope so that he stopped and pretended to look at the view.

"Just think," he murmured hoarsely, "there were once buffalo herds that stretched from here to the western horizon . . ."

"Are there none left?" Sarah asked politely as we waited.

"Very few around here now. They say there are still some in the north." He paused to hack discreetly into his hollowed hand again. "We have closed the curtain on the first act of an epic play."

"What will be the second act?" Sarah asked.

"Regulated settlement," he replied, and he walked toward the campfire where the general's entourage gathered.

The sun hadn't touched the horizon yet, and I saw from our elevation that the burial detail had started pushing wheelbarrow loads of bones and trash and dumping them over the riverbank, while Joe Minelli had already dug a hole in the ground and was setting limestone rocks for the monument's foundation.

Part of the battlefield looked a little better already. I had a momentary thought about what might happen if battlefields were never touched, never cleaned up, but preserved in situ, maybe varnish the bones once in a while to keep them from rotting from the weather. But leave the skulls bashed in and gaping, leave the finger bones clutched tightly together, leave the horses' bones where they neighed their death screams and fell. Leave the bayonet between the ribs, the revolver in the hand, leave the craters mortar bombs made and the splintered bones like daisy petals lying around them.

Then guide the children through, try to explain it rationally.

Mercifully, this train of thought was interrupted by a rider dressed in blue galloping toward us from the northeast. Bent low over his sorrel's neck, his gold epaulets and the braid on his Kossuth hat shone brightly.

There was no one chasing him.

"Courier coming," I said, and the people gathered around the fire turned to look.

August Hamilton Root muttered, "Cross your fingers, General."

"I daresay it's as important to you as to me," the general growled, gnawing at a half-roasted chunk of buffalo rib.

"As in profit or loss." Root tried to smile, but his nerves were too tight, and his hatred for the fat man was beginning to show through his chubby, ebullient features.

Why didn't he say "in victory or defeat"? I wondered as the rider skidded his foam-slopped mount showily into camp, dismounted, saluted, and handed over an oilskin packet to the general.

"General Sherman's compliments, sir," the courier snapped out.

The general lifted his fat right hand, waggled it near

his head as a salute, and grumbled, "Took you long enough."

"Yes, sir," the courier said. "I left Ellsworth this morning as soon as the telegram arrived."

"What the hell you want? A medal?" the general snarled, his attention now on fumbling the oilskin open.

The trooper flushed but was smart enough to keep quiet.

The general's pudgy fingers worked futilely at the bowknot until he abruptly shoved the packet into his son Billy's hands and growled, "Open the goddamned thing and read it to me."

Nervously Billy managed to undo the knot and extract the yellow page.

The sun was setting on the horizon like an iron cannonball heated to cherry red, and Billy coughed and paused to clear his throat.

"Jesus H. Christ!" the general said disgustedly.

"Brigadier General Frederick Falls; In accordance with the instructions given you last May twelfth in the War Office, you are hereby ordered to take command of the Department of Dakota Territory, with the rank of Major General. In concert with Generals Crook and Terry, proceed henceforth as advised by the Commander-in-Chief. Signed, William Tecumseh Sherman, Commanding General."

The rigid, stiff silence that followed was quickly broken by August Root crying out, "Bravo!" and that brought on the hurried congratulations of Doc

Cadwell, Billy, and even Curt Sickle, who had drifted in quiet as smoke.

Gerald Barr stared at the general, his mouth partly open in surprise, a strange look in his eyes that lasted only a second before his face folded upward in a crooked grin.

"Anyone who can make two stars deserves the presidency, too," he said.

I looked over at Skofer, his jaws clenched together, shaking his head in disbelief.

"Presidency!"

Sure enough, I thought, they're grooming him to replace Grant! This was the reason for all the grand fiction that Gerald Barr was feeding the eastern newspapers. This was the reason for the commemoration of the battlefield. This was why he'd been given the second star and an army to exterminate the last of the hostiles in the north.

The general didn't bother to acknowledge the congratulations and scattered applause as he tore a chunk of fat off the rib with his teeth, greedily chewed the grease out of it, and swallowed with pleasure. He wore a biblike towel tied around his neck to protect his tunic, and after he'd tossed the bone into the fire he wiped his fingers and his bearded lips with the bib, then looked up at the standing people with amused contempt.

"Yes, the party wants me," he growled. "And you'll all go along with me if you can follow orders. I might as well tell you, Grant and Sherman and I met at the

White House last May. We discussed whether it would be politically valuable to force the Sioux into battle and destroy them. This message merely confirms that Grant finally made up his mind to go ahead with it."

Now it was Sarah with her eyes puzzled and her mouth half open in shocked wonderment. She couldn't believe this was how the military hand fit the civilian glove, couldn't believe they'd connive to annihilate an Indian nation so that another general could be elected president.

"We seem to be running with some pretty high-tailed polecats," I murmured to Skofer, and after an orderly had fetched the general a chunk of roasted buffalo tongue I wandered over to the fire and cut myself a slab off the juicy hump. Skofer managed to find a tin plate and serve a chunk to Sarah before spearing his own.

We moved back as the sun plopped like a broken bubble under the horizon while the others hovered around the general like they were cold and he was the fire.

The general knew it all. His little pig eyes read them, filed the report, and went on from there.

"Get the hell away from me," he snarled, washing down the roast tongue with a glass of brandy.

The group faded away like autumn leaves before a gust of wind. August Root smiled sickly, furtively touched his open shirt cuffs, and murmured vaguely, "Damn, I've lost my cuff links." Then he ran his hand down to his crotch to feel if his fly was unbuttoned while announcing, "My, what a beautiful sunset."

Lieutenant Billy Falls turned and walked jerkily over toward the ambulance like he had important business.

Young Doc Cadwell fluffed up his thistledown sideburns and arched his eyebrows before drifting away.

I saw Snow hunkered down by the front wheel of the daugherty frowning at the roasting meat he'd brought in.

Gerald Barr put a handkerchief to his mouth and moved after the doctor when the general bellowed, "Barr, bring your sketch pad."

"Yes, sir," Barr answered quickly, and he went off toward the daugherty.

Curt Sickle, tall and thin, moved gracefully to the fire, sliced off some of the backstrap, and faded away slicker'n calf splatter.

Sarah Duffy sat on a camp stool that Skofer had found for her, staring at the general like a bird hypnotized by a snake.

When Gerald Barr returned with his pad of stiff paper and took the silver pen and ink case out of his coat pocket, the general said, "You're slow, Barr. The slow ones lose the race."

"I'm not feeling so well today, General," Barr said apologetically.

"In the army there are no excuses. I want you to make a portrait that shows power and wisdom, honesty and sympathy. After you've finished, write a story to accompany it that describes my successes as a military man and statesman and family man. I want it to go out at daybreak with the courier."

"That's quite an order for one night, General."

"You can be replaced, Barr," the general said plain out.

"Of course, General. I just said it was a tall order." Barr's bashful, crooked grin was beginning to fall apart. His hand was unsteady as he made cross-hatched shadows on the paper. "But of course I'll do it, just like I've always done."

"This will anticipate the bigger story concerning the commemoration of the battlefield and the land preserve around it, I suppose." Root moved in smoothly.

"Yes, but the problem with that story is that Sheridan will hog it." The general smiled. "This way we beat him to it by two days."

"Very shrewd, General," Root said. "I believe we've got it all wrapped up, then."

What the hell was wrapped up? I wondered. What kind of code was Root talking through his cherubic mouth and meaning through his foxy eyes?

"That will do, Root. You may be the Lion of the Prairie, but you talk too goddamned much," the general said sharply.

"I only meant—"

"Just shut the hell up!" the general thundered. "I've had enough of your schemes for now."

Before Root could protest or apologize the general yelled, "Lieutenant!"

"Here, sir." Billy Falls came running and stood at attention.

"How would you like to be Secretary of War and put this little monkey to running around the Capitol carrying dirty little pieces of paper from one office to another?" The general, swaying back and forth and eyeing Root, guffawed.

"Whatever you say, sir," Billy stammered.

"It may just come to that." The general took another drink of the amber brandy and waggled his index finger at the white-faced Root. "Get out!"

Root's half-closed eyes gleamed like red-hot rivets as he nodded and murmured, "Your servant, sir."

"You pitiful excuse for a soldier . . ." The general looked over at his son disgustedly. "Go sit on a cannon."

"Yes, sir." Billy Falls stepped away into the gathering shadows.

I wondered if the general was drunk on his newest success or on the Spanish brandy that spilled down his wattles.

He closed his little pig eyes like he was going to sleep.

"Sickle!" he yelled suddenly.

"I'm here," Sickle answered, drifting closer.

"I hear you're a bounty hunter." The general glared at the slim gunman. "I hear you kill people for money."

"I'm not arguin', General."

"I'm informed that a certain Chicago cattle broker who happened to become crippled in the war has put a price on my head."

"I haven't heard that story," Sickle said softly.

"I've been advised to the contrary." The general leaned forward, his voice cracking like a bullwhip.

"And I warn you now, Mr. Sickle, I have the ways and means not only to protect myself, but to make you disappear from the face of the earth."

"You're talkin' to the wrong man, General." Sickle shrugged his thin shoulders.

"Bah!" The general sneered and waved his hand in dismissal. "You're a born back-shooting poltroon."

Sickle didn't argue about it, but the color was up in his face, and there was a glitter in his dark eyes that spelled menace.

"Snow!" the general bellowed. "You goddamned halfbreed ingrate! Get over here. I'm not finished by a long shot."

Snow appeared silently on moccasined feet and leaned toward the general as if he were afraid he might miss a word.

"You've been prowling around camp like a thief in the night. I don't know what's the matter with you, but I've had a bellyful of your sneaking ways. Your orders are to have at least one young buffalo cow, two deer, and three antelope ready for our guests the day after tomorrow."

"Maybe so," Snow muttered.

"Don't say maybe so to me, you stinking dog turd!" The general bellowed so loudly, Snow backed up from the force of it.

Snow's mouth worked, but the words didn't come out. His eyes flashed but looked down at the ground. In the terrorized silence he backed out of the firelight.

"I'm beginning to enjoy this," the general boomed with a down-bent grin. "Who's next needs straighten-

ing out? The doctor! Step up and take your medicine!"
The general's off-center laugh made the back of my
neck tingle. The damn fool was roaring drunk, but he
had everyone so buffaloed, no one could hold him
down.

Dr. Martin Cadwell reluctantly stepped forward
and said in a quiet, bedside voice, "Sir, I think you
should rest."

"I'll rest after I've got my troops shaped up!" the
general bellowed again, then he steadied down. "Doctor, I've been watching you minister to the young
recruits. I do not approve of doctors with mincing
manners making calf eyes at the dregs of humanity
they give me nowadays to turn into fighting men."

"Please—" The doctor's face turned pale, his voice
faint.

"No pleases!" The general grimaced. "I am set to
see you court-martialed and dishonorably discharged."

"There's no evidence—" the doctor squeaked.

"You should never have attempted to approach the
lieutenant, Doctor. He tells me everything." The
general sounded like Jehovah sending thunderous
threats down from smoke-blackened heavens.

The doctor put his hands over his face and stumbled away.

I thought I was ready for him when he yelled out my
name.

"Yes, sir." I stepped into the firelight.

"You're a former cavalry captain under the traitorous Jeb Stuart, a coward of the first water."

"We never slaughtered women and children in their beds like you did here," I responded with as much quiet dignity as I could muster.

"That's enough of your insolence, mister," he roared. "Sergeant Price and Corporal Mulholland, you two stand on either side of this traitor, and if he opens his mouth without my permission, stick a fist in it."

They moved quickly, as if they'd had their orders earlier, and I began to think the general wasn't as drunk as he looked.

"You're finished here, Benbow," he said slowly. "I'm going to teach you a few tricks you never learned down in corn-pone country, then I'm going to—"

I held up my hand, palm toward him, and he looked at me with disbelief.

"What is it?" he growled after a moment of thinking it over.

"We found the lower village," I said. "It shows you ran off and left Company A."

"That's a goddamned lie!" he roared. "You rotten rebel, you can't touch my reputation."

I shook my head and shrugged.

"I believe he's correct, General," Sarah Duffy said clearly. "You abandoned them."

"Be quiet, woman." The general meant to bull it through. "No one has studied that site yet."

"You pulled your troops back to slaughter a thousand Indian ponies while Company A was fighting for their lives," I said, and the sergeant's big fist crashed against my cheekbone. I went down on one knee and tried to keep from falling over.

"Lieutenant Falls!" the general raged, "bring my bronze plaque and read it again."

"Yessir."

As we waited the ponderous, brutish hulk leaned forward and stared hard at each person around the fire.

"You miserable people will learn the rigors of discipline, or I will cast you aside. Major General Frederick Falls has a mission of leadership against the enemies of this great country. You will give me your best, or you will go under."

A stick flared in the fire. In the shadows I saw Joe Minelli's face limned like a death mask, and I suddenly understood part of the puzzle. The general's arrogance and assurance and his contempt for weaker beings was just the surface of the evil.

"You killed Johnny Minelli!" I popped off, forgetting about the sergeant.

This time I ended up on hands and knees, shaking the bell-ringers out of my head, but glad I'd dug out the simple truth.

The general pulled his head back imperiously so that his grim jaw angled upward like a howitzer ready to fire at the moon, and his voice grated with righteousness and certitude. "Benbow, a snotty kid provoked me with his insolent impudence once too often."

I'd said all I wanted to say.

The general looked off at his ambulance, where a lantern showed through the curtains.

"What the hell is taking so long?" he demanded loudly. "On the double, Lieutenant!"

"Sorry, sir," Billy Falls stammered, coming back into the firelight empty-handed. "It seems to be gone."

"Gone?" the general bellowed, his eyes bulging like he'd been shot in the back of the head. "Gone? That's not possible!"

"The box is empty, sir," Billy Falls said tremulously.

"It's not important anyway if it's all a lie," Sarah Duffy spoke out clearly.

The general's face turned purple as a damson plum as he rocked up to his feet and grabbed his son by the shoulder to steady himself.

Turning to the sergeant, he said, "No one is permitted to leave camp without my written permission."

"Yessir," the sergeant said.

Facing the group now like a bull backed into a mesquite patch, the general glared around and growled, "That plaque had better be on my doorstep the first thing in the morning, or there will be a great deal of god-awful misery among you. I will leave the lantern lighted."

=== 5 ===

I WAS DREAMING ABOUT DRIVING A STAGECOACH THROUGH mountain country with Skofer riding shotgun, only he had a quart of Old Bulldog instead of the shotgun, and between drinks he was singing something about Suzy, little Suzy:

> "What is the news?
> The geese are going barefoot
> Because they have no shoes . . ."

Then he dropped the bottle and howled like a coyote bitch in rut, and kept on howling, only it was changed to something new and human, and I thought it must be reveille, but there was no bugle call that morning.

"Doctor! Call the doctor!"

I was in my boots and hat before Skofer snorted and pawed at his face.

The howl came from up on the rise, and as I charged up the slope I saw Billy Falls standing on the iron let-down step of the general's ambulance.

There were others coming on the run as Billy Falls grabbed my arm and looked at me with shocked eyes, his face pasty white, his mouth still open.

"The general?" I guessed, trying to see into the open side door.

He nodded dumbly, and I pushed on by.

A blanket half covered the bulky general, who was clad in a voluminous red flannel nightshirt. One look and I knew there was no need for a doctor.

The steel-bladed battle axe lay by the general's head, which had been severed from the body by a flurry of powerful blows delivered so fast that one had missed and sliced off the protruding chin, exposing the roots of his lower incisors.

The first whack must have been the most accurate, the killer driving the blade straight down, probably with both hands, cleaving through the larynx and pharynx, which silenced Falls forever. Panicked by the still-living, thrashing body, the axe man had swung again and again until both carotid arteries had been sundered, the vertebral joint and the major ligaments bisected.

Blood spattered the canvas curtain by the bed and clotted the bedclothes in viscid puddles.

I looked over the rest of the living space, but there

was nothing hanging on the wall except the general's looped-up Kossuth hat with three ostrich feathers sewn into the band. They looked sillier than ever with the general's vacant eyes staring at them.

"What's happened?" came the peach-fuzz voice of Dr. Cadwell behind me.

I moved aside. "Somebody chopped him."

"Dear Heaven! No wonder Billy was screaming!" Cadwell babbled, not bothering to touch the body. "I thought someone had found my scalpels, then I was afraid someone had used them, but this is monstrous!"

I backed toward the door and stepped out into the pale light of dawn. Billy looked at me, hoping I would tell him he was having a bad dream.

I shook my head. It wasn't a dream. His father was deader'n hell.

"Come have a cup of coffee," I said.

He followed me over to the portable field kitchen where the black cooks had placed a big enamelware pot near the fire.

While one of them poured our coffee the other rolled his eyes and asked softly, "Should we make breakfast, sir?"

"Yes, Private," Billy said. "We will carry on as usual."

I sat at the table across from him and asked, "Can you talk about it?"

"Father told me to get up early and come see about the plaque. He said to wake him if it wasn't there."

"Was it?"

"No. There was nothing outside. Then I thought someone might have slid it through the door or pushed it through one of the side flaps, so I went inside and—" He knotted his fists and set the white knuckles against his jawbones to hold back his emotions.

"Did you touch anything? Move something? Take something?" I asked.

"I blew out the lantern, that's all. Why?"

"Wide Bear's relics, except for the battle axe, are gone."

"I don't know." He shook his head. "My bootjack is missing, but it'll turn up somewhere. Otherwise, I'm completely in the dark."

"You're the senior officer present. You're going to have to take command and make decisions."

"Good Lord, Sheridan and all the brass are coming, expecting a big victory show . . ." he muttered, knocking his fists together.

I thought that was a healthy sign.

"Nothing much has changed except you'll have an extra grave," I said. "They can have their show. They'll just have to find a new general."

"It'll be Crook," Billy Falls said. "Father hates— hated—him. Said George was too timid."

The whole scattered-out camp was wide awake by now, and men clustered around the general's ambulance, talking quietly. I saw Skofer across the way and Curt Sickle leaning against the front wheel of the ambulance.

64

"First thing to think about is getting Doc to prepare him for burial," I said. "Nobody will go to work until the routine gets started."

"No, the first thing on my mind is to find the man that did this," Billy said, his jaw firming up as he looked directly at me.

I didn't volunteer, so he went on with his thinking. "Father said you were some kind of detective . . ."

"I'm a brand inspector and stock detective, that's all." I nodded.

"Then I'm putting you in charge of finding the killer of my father," Billy said flat out.

"No, thanks." I shook my head. "I've got other fish to fry."

"I'll double your regular wage and put up a thousand dollars reward for bringing that man to justice," he said harshly.

About then I thought Billy was one of the best liars I'd ever seen, or he really had nothing to do with his father's murder. He had plenty of reasons for chopping the general's head off, but there was no blood on him, and whoever had used that feathered axe would have been awash in it.

"No offense, Lieutenant," I said, "but I had a notion you'd had a bellyfull of being treated like a yeller dog."

He looked down at the table, shook his head, and, with his voice cracking, he murmured, "I always thought that someday I would measure up and make him proud. . . ."

What it amounted to, General Falls had been eating up his son's life along with everything else he could get close to.

I ran it through my mind again and shook my head. "If I don't turn up the killer by the time of the dedication of the monument, I'll have to quit, and you'll owe me nothing."

"Done," he said, rising, and as he strode over to the ambulance the clustered groups of men moved out of the way.

"Dr. Cadwell!"

The doctor poked his head out of the side door and said, "Yes, sir?"

"Prepare the general's body for burial. I want a decent coffin for him."

"Gosh, Billy," the doctor said hesitantly, "I don't know where—"

"See that it's done," the lieutenant snapped, "and be quick about it."

"Yessir," the doctor said with surprise, and he saluted, but Billy had already done an about-face and said sharply to the men lounging about, "We have less than three days to get ready. I expect every one of you to do more than the usual duty. I want the field clean. I want the grave markers set properly. I want the monument and flagpole in place, and the flag will fly at half mast. Understood?"

"Yessir."

In a minute the only people left in the area were Joe Minelli, August Root, and Gerald Barr.

"What is it, Mr. Minelli?" Billy asked.

"You got the plaque?" Minelli asked, looking at the ground.

"No. The plaque is gone. Just build the monument according to plan, and we'll send another one out later on."

"Yes, sir," Minelli said, and he backed away, his manner respectful. His big, scaly hands were clean, but there had been murder in his heart last night.

"Billy—" Root started off on the wrong foot.

"Just a second, Mr. Root. Please address me by my rank," young Falls said firmly.

Root's genial smile faded, his eyes sparked, and he snapped, "Don't get on your high horse with me, sonny. I'm the man who gives the promotions, remember?"

"You will call me Lieutenant," Billy came back at him louder and harder, "and you can stick your promotions up your nose. Your duty here is to deliver the eulogy. It had better be good."

"Look, Lieutenant, I understand"—Root fell back to his familiar slimy soft-soap patter—"I know you're under a terrible strain, you've suffered a great personal loss, but we have to carry on . . . we want to remember your father and I had a deal. . . ."

"I haven't time now," Billy said. "I know nothing of your deal. I'm not a party to it."

"I'll explain it to you later, then."

Billy Falls had already turned toward Gerald Barr, in effect dismissing Root.

Root had hated the general as much as anyone, maybe more. The general had told him he was just an errand boy for more powerful people, and it hadn't set well with the two-faced, split-tongued politician.

He could have washed off the blood and changed his clothes easily by now. He was plenty strong enough to swing the battle axe, but why would he take Wide Bear's relics?

"How can I help, Lieutenant?" Barr asked, his hound-dog eyes underlined with gray, the rose on his cheekbones brighter.

"Write the straight story of the general's murder and attach the portrait you did last night to it so that I can send it off with the courier as soon as possible."

"I'm sorry, Lieutenant, that sketch didn't come out right what with all the uproar. I tore it up."

"They can use an old one, then," Billy said quickly. "Just write the story."

"Should I suggest he was killed by a vengeful Indian?"

"I said write it straight. The unknown murderer is at large, that's all we have for sure. Sam Benbow is in charge of the investigation if you need more details."

Maybe there was a renegade Indian hiding along the river who wanted the relics back and wanted revenge for the Wild River massacre. I wondered. The battle axe would suit him well. A quiet, stealthy approach in the night . . . I shook my head.

Lieutenant Billy Falls walked back across the camp, seeing that everyone was busy.

I was still thinking about a renegade Indian doing the killing . . . after all, he could have been watching from outside the light of the campfire. Could have seen the general half carried to his ambulance, could have slipped through the camp when the fire died down.

I was still deep in sorting out myth from reality when the soft, low voice of Sarah Duffy broke through.

"Mr. Benbow, I believe I heard Lieutenant Falls say you were in charge of the investigation . . ."

I turned around, studied the gentle curves of her face, and looked into her dark eyes. "I hope you're not going to confess," I said.

"Me?" She shook her head.

"He was pretty rough on you last night," I suggested.

"He was rough on you and everyone else."

"Yes," I had to agree, "there's no shortage of enemies with the ability to do it, including me."

Like a bee finds a flower, Skofer came buzzing along, trying to look like he was on serious business.

"Good morning, Sarah," he greeted her. "You can see we're called upon to do our duty."

"I understand"—she nodded—"but aren't you a suspect like anyone else?"

"You're not a suspect, Sarah!" Skofer melted under the warmth of her open gaze. "Heck, you couldn't have swung that axe."

"Any day a farm girl can't swing an axe will be a

frosty day down below." She smiled and lifted her large, capable, and work-hardened hands. "These are the hands of a working lady."

I noticed a small cut at the base of her thumb.

"I still can't think you'd have the stomach for it, Sarah." Skofer gazed at her reverently.

"How many times have I axed a chicken's head off?" She smiled. "How many hogs have I gutted out and scalded? How many lambs have I stabbed in the throat and hung from the gambrel hooks to bleed? Ah, Skofer, my hands have been bloodied many, many times."

"That's different," he insisted. "This was a man."

"But I never regarded that boar hog as human. He needed killing more than any ewe lamb or red rooster," she said somberly.

"Skofe," I interrupted, "we're supposed to be keepin' an eye on that nester down river."

He looked at me like a punished pup.

"You mean you want me to leave this little lady at the mercy of a murderer?" he whimpered.

"That's what I'm askin' you to do," I said, "and if I can earn the reward while you're gone, we can be on our way to San Juan Bautista tomorrow."

"What do you want me to tell this Mordecai Jones?" He gave up.

"Tell him to hold his fire and stay out of the way of any longhorns crossing the river."

"He already knows that—"

"I figure he's got a short memory," I said. "Just tell

him he can't do what he's tryin' to do. Tell him the railroad's moving on west toward Dodge City, and it won't be long before the problem will solve itself."

"Do or die, I shall try," he said. "And you be careful, Sarah." He took her hand gallantly and kissed the back of it.

"What a fine gentleman," Sarah said wistfully, watching Skofer bowlegging it over to our camp. Then she cocked her ear and listened to the wind and something else. "Whatever is that?"

I listened closely and caught the words on the breeze.

". . . One year ago today, this pleasant, pastoral scene of arboreal splendor was riven with the hearty shouts of brave soldiers and the blood-curdling war cries of hostile savages . . ."

"I'd guess that's the honorable August Root practicing his speech," I said.

"If you'll excuse me." Sarah smiled at me, and I could understand why Skofer went dough-legged when she looked at him. "This is my last clean dress. I've got to do my washing."

I thought of asking her to do mine, too, but instead I said, "I'll be around, crossing names off my list."

"Have you scratched mine off yet?" She turned back.

"No, ma'am. You aren't even on it, so far."

"Thank you," she said. "Who's next?"

"I figure to parley with that bird that seems to be taggin' your skirt a lot."

"And who would that be?" she laughed. "You don't mean Skofer—"

"No, ma'am, that other jasper named Curt Sickle."

Sickle stood in the shade of a grove of cottonwoods upriver, his black gelding picketed off in the deep grass. He had a six-gun in either hand when I saw him, and I froze.

His back was to me, and he hadn't heard me coming up because of the soft silt footing and the murmuring of the flowing river.

He settled the Colts in their scabbards, relaxed, scuffed the dirt with his boot, then suddenly whirled half a turn to the left, drawing the blue steel Colts as he shifted.

He was so fast, I didn't see a pause when his hands grabbed the walnut grips and lifted. Generally there's about half a second lost there when your hands reverse their motion, but he didn't lose anything.

Again he settled the Colts and held his hands up high. I noticed he kept his knees slightly bent. Then, on some sort of invisible signal, he leapt to the right off the left foot, the knees uncorking to give him the spring, and at the same time the Colts flashed out and up.

He could draw quicker'n I can spit, faster'n chain lightning with a link snapped.

I backed off slowly, thinking if it ever came to a powder-burning contest with him, I'd have to pray he missed the first two shots.

Reaching the grassland, I yelled, "Hey, anybody lose a black mule?"

He came out of the trees like a dark shadow. All in black. He stopped, put his hands on his thin hips, and glared at me.

"That's a good horse, Benbow. What the hell you want?"

"Little parley." I smiled. "Nothin' much."

"About the general?"

"That's the main subject," I said, walking toward him and finding a handy old cottonwood log to sit on.

"He made a lot of unfriendly noise last night," Sickle said. "I don't know why he picked on me."

"Sickle, you know that for a while after the war I sort of went crazy and wasted some good time hangin' around El Paso and such places."

I didn't mention that it was what I found in Colorado right after the war that drove me crazy, because I still couldn't bear to think about it.

"I saw you down there. I was still a greenhorn kid, but you were the boss billy goat in the cabbage patch, just shootin' people every which way."

"I guess those days just won't stay buried and gone." I shook my head. "I'm not so awful proud of that time in my life."

"Hell, why not? I always figured you were the best, and my whole ambition was to get ready to take you down."

"What happened was that old geezer that took up with me, him and me'd rode together in the war and afterward, he come lookin'. When he saw how it was with me, he talked me into ridin' out to California with him."

"They ain't mean enough out there in California," Curt Sickle grumbled. "I looked it over once. Too soft. I like it where you don't know from one minute to the next who's goin' to get himself shot."

"I'm just tellin' you this so you'll know my cards," I said apologetically. "I'm not lookin' for no high stakes shootout with anybody, I'm just interested in finding out who killed the general."

"Old age melted your backbone, Benbow?" he answered. "Hell, I always figured we'd have a go sometime."

"Sorry, those days been torn out of the almanac and throwed away." I shook my head. "I'd probably blow my foot off if I tried to draw this old hogleg in a hurry."

"How many you think I've put down?" he asked, like he'd finally found somebody who understood him.

"Over twenty?"

"Hell's fire, twenty ain't nothin'!" He kind of laughed like he had the hiccups. "I'm up to forty-three now, not countin' my cousin."

"Why don't you count your cousin?" I asked, picking my teeth with a wild oat straw.

"I used a hatchet on her when she threatened to tattletale to the folks." He shook his head like he was sorry. "Had to live off the land after that, and I was just fourteen."

"It's a hard life." I sighed sympathetically. "Was there anything in what the general was sayin' last night?"

"I'd give a posy to find out how he got on to it." Sickle nodded and settled down to sit on his heels. "The old bronco that hired me must've run off at the mouth to somebody."

"Just a matter of simple revenge?" I murmured, finally getting the shred of last night's buffalo out from between my back molars. It tasted sour, and I spit it out.

"I met this wooden-legged cattle broker in Ellsworth. He pegged along pretty good, but one day he recognized the general going by in his ambulance, and foamed at the mouth. Seems like early in the war this broker was Fall's captain, and he was leading a skirmish line up a hill when somebody shot him in the leg from behind. He claimed it wasn't an accident. Falls took his rank and moved over to Washington."

"I guess that'd be enough to remember a while. What does a simple killin' cost nowadays?"

"He give me a hundred down and promised a hundred after I did the job. Goddamn it!"

"So you're out a hundred"—I commiserated with him—"unless you chopped him."

"Not my style." He shook his head. "You feel up to fightin' me now?"

"Oh, my, no." I shuddered. "I'm lookin' for an old front porch with a rockin' chair and a fat tomcat purrin' on it."

"Goddamn it, that's a hell of a note." He frowned.

"The whole damn world is goin' wrong. I've gotten so low I have to practice on cottonwood trees."

"Ain't that the truth." I nodded sadly and climbed to my feet.

Suddenly he came alert and stepped backwards on his toes, his knees bent, his torso arched forward like spring steel, his hands spread out and poised.

I cocked my head and looked at him, surprised. "See there, you got me cold before I could even think shoot. Gettin' hot, ain't it?"

"Go ahead, big man," he said tightly. "You pick the time."

"Hell, it's damn near high noon, no wonder it's warmin' up," I said, lifting up my hat with my right hand and running my shirtsleeve over my forehead.

"You yella-gutted lawman, try it!" he snapped, still keyed tight as a Scotch maiden's crotch on a stormy night.

I brought the hat over my chest and took the left side of the brim in my left hand so it looked like I was a Mexican farmer asking the boss for a spare hatful of beans.

"Simmer down, Curt," I murmured abjectly, "we're all just mortal clay that cometh and goeth. . . ."

I had the eerie thought just then that Skofer would be proud of me for saying it that way, but the idea didn't last long as I looked into Sickle's hatchet-thin face and, on the fuzzy fringe of my vision, saw his shoulders and arms relax and start to come down.

The hat in my left hand raked him across the eyes so

fast he didn't see my shoulder shift and my right fist crossing over.

A flap and a crunch, and he dropped facedown to the ground. I kind of hated to do it because he was smaller'n me, but then so is a rattlesnake smaller'n me.

I lifted his short-barreled forty-fours, swung out the cylinders, and punched out the cartridges into my hand. He clawed spasmodically at the grass, and I put my number twelve boot on the back of his neck.

"Listen here, sonny, you remember I'm faster'n you any time, any place. You try bushwhackin' me a mile away, I'm still goin' to be faster'n a lizard after a pissant. Understood?"

Still facedown, he nodded.

"You don't have any business here anymore. You want to ride back down to El Paso and shoot old drunks? Say yes."

He nodded a yes in the dust.

= 6 =

IT DID NOT HAPPEN IN A DAY OR A NIGHT. THE BATTLE OF Wild River resulted from three score and three decades of greed, treachery, and deceit that would shame even Machiavelli in their cupidity and, yea! voracity . . ."

The keening prairie wind carried Root's high nasal voice across the rise, and I shook my head and smiled at Sarah Duffy.

"Still practicin'," she said.

"Just gettin' warmed up." I nodded. "I haven't figured out which side he's talkin' about, have you?"

"I suppose it's whichever he wants it to be."

She'd let the shawl come down over her shoulders, and her loosened dark brown hair drifted on the whining wind. Her eyes were distant, as if she couldn't make up her mind about something.

"I'm going down by the river and make sure my brother did not die there," she murmured hesitantly.

"If you want someone along, I'm volunteerin'."

"It's so different than I thought it would be." Her strong shoulders sagged. "Somehow I thought it would all be neat and tidy, the way they're trying to make it now."

"War is about as untidy an enterprise as there is," I said.

"If the general had brought their bodies back, it would have at least been honorable." She frowned.

"The general was not an honorable man," I said, thinking I ought to be asking questions of Minelli, Snow, Doc Cadwell, Barr, and Root. But instead I meant to help a lady sort through a couple acres of bones.

"Let's get it over with," she said quietly. "I do not believe Tom fell there. I believe he still lives somewhere. I must not get faint-hearted now that I can prove it."

"I hope you're right," I said, helping her up to the buckboard seat.

I rode the steeldust alongside as she drove the long way around the rise down to the ruined village on the lower river.

Off in the shadows of the cottonwoods I saw Doc Cadwell carrying a white flour sack stuffed full. He stopped, looked right and left, then with both hands heaved the sack out into the river.

Up to the right the burial detail loaded the wheelbarrows and pushed the leftovers of battle across to the riverbank, lifted the hickory handles, and sent the load of weathered bones and rags down the steep bank into the river, where it would be washed along to the Arkansas, on to the Missouri, and then empty into the Mississippi. In a year or two maybe the remains of the Battle of Wild River would be filling up the Gulf of Mexico below New Orleans.

"Your only brother?" I asked, passing the time.

"Yes." She nodded. "I guess that's what makes him so special."

"If he's here, it won't be pretty," I said, not liking any part of this. She might have wrung a lot of chicken necks, I thought, but we weren't going to be looking at chicken bones.

"I can do it," she said firmly.

"Maybe it'd be better if I went ahead. If I found a tin front tooth, would you take my word for it?"

"Much obliged, Sam," she said, setting her jaw, "but it's my job, and I'm going to do it."

She pulled up the team at the edge of the fallen-down lodges and climbed down from the buckboard.

We walked from east to west upriver, finding nothing of significance, but at the northern edge of the camp, which bore the brunt of Company A's attack, the outlying teepees had been completely knocked down, and there the bones started.

Gnawed by coyotes and wolves, parts of skeletons lay jumbled in an arc like a chalky line marking the defense of the village.

You could say pretty sure which were Indians and which were soldiers.

The arcing chalk line was mainly made up of Indians that could be identified by remaining copper bracelets and stone ornaments.

I counted sixteen skulls that I thought were Kiowas in that line of defense.

The company had gotten off at least one volley before whirling their horses and trying to retreat.

But there were less than twenty of them, and the Indians had known they were coming. The Kiowa's arc, taking Company A on the flank, had pinched them against the river, and the troopers died in a ragged line trying to break free.

There were still plenty of tattered blue rags about, but the carbines and six-shooters had been taken by surviving Kiowas before they headed north.

Mixed in with the human remains were heavier horse bones dragged apart and scattered by scavengers.

I moved a shade faster than Sarah, so that I was a few steps ahead as we crisscrossed the flat area next to the river.

The skeletons became more separated, showing how they'd been thinned out by maybe a hundred warriors.

A genuine battle had gone on there, and the general hadn't heard it, didn't even know it was happening.

Maybe he knew and didn't care. It was only a company half depleted by desertion.

I saw the white gloss off to the left in the willows as I worked carefully back and forth across the field, identifying troopers by remnants of insignia and patches of faded blue flannel; and when I came to the end, where the last man fell, I had counted eighteen naked, sometimes knocked-in skulls that would have to be gathered up and buried along with the others.

How could the army historian Gerald Barr account for them in his report?

"Eighteen troopers of Company A were lured into a trap by the treacherous Wide Bear. . . ."

Sarah came up alongside me, her face pale, her eyes somber, but she forced a small smile. "I haven't seen a sign of him anywhere." She looked at me hopefully for confirmation.

Right then I could have said "me neither," and she could have gone through the rest of her life waiting for Tommy to come back home. I thought about it enough to weigh the right and wrong before saying, "There's something over in that willow patch. I hope it's just a horse's aitch bone. Would you rather call it a day?"

"Sam, I came for the truth," she said tiredly.

I led the way through the brush, sometimes forcing a trail through the tight branches, and stepped into what once might have been a deer's hidden sleeping place.

Lying facedown in that small open space were the almost untouched remains of a trooper. His boots were cracked and curled, but the spurs were still buckled onto the heels.

The gal's leg was silver, the garter and slipper gold.

"That's enough," I said.

"Not quite," she said angrily, tears running down her cheeks.

She leaned over and touched the skull, which still bore patches of reddish brown hair, knelt, and with both trembling hands turned the skull so that the empty eye sockets stared skyward.

The lower jawbone slipped aside, but the arch of teeth in the upper jaw was perfect except for the left front incisor of tarnished pewter.

As she started to slump over I grabbed her under the arms and lifted her to her feet.

"All right," I said harshly, "you saw it. Now let me do the rest."

The hardness of my voice penetrated the fog overcoming her mind, and she set her jaw so tight the muscles knotted and her lips compressed into a thin, pale scar.

She broke loose from my arms and stumbled out of the willows to the flat ground.

I followed along to where she stood in the open, her head bowed, her shoulders shaking.

Wrapping my arms around her, I said, "Go ahead, let it loose."

A great sob burst from her throat, and tears poured from her eyes. She huddled against me like a child, sobbing and bawling her heart out.

Gradually her great gusting sobs subsided and dwindled away to simple tears and sniffles, and then I heard a horse coming down the slope.

Over her shoulder I saw Snow riding his pinto toward us, his carbine across the bow of his saddle.

"Trouble?" he asked, his dark, pockmarked face flat, his eyes hidden.

She stepped back, and I said, "We found the remains of her brother over in the willows." I faced her and said, "Please let me handle it."

"All right," she said, looking at the ground. "What does it matter now?"

I walked her over to the buckboard and took a folded-up piece of light canvas out of the back. "Just wait here. I won't be long."

I didn't wait for an answer but legged it back to the willows where Snow was bending over the bones.

"Horse fell on him," he said, his index finger almost touching the broken pieces of the right femur, including the hip socket and pelvis. "Crawled in here and hid."

The skull was intact; there were no other broken or damaged bones.

"What do you think?" I asked, afraid to admit what was obvious.

"A break like that—" He shook his head. "It swells up and hurts too much."

"You're saying he crawled in here and couldn't crawl out."

"See the willows . . ." He pointed at the gray, dead branches where the bark had been gnawed off.

"That willow bark killed the pain," he said.

"I think he was just hungry."

"He starved to death." The halfbreed nodded.

"Maybe took a week," I muttered, feeling sick.

"That general"—Snow shook his head again—"he fooled everybody but me."

"How do you mean?" I asked, spreading out the tarp and carefully laying the bones of Tom Duffy on it.

"He was yellow all the way through," he said.

"That's too simple," I said, adding the still-integumented vertebra to the pile. "He was a raging bull last night."

"Sure, because he'd worked it around so you were all afraid of him and he could kick everybody in the butt."

"Did you kill him?" I asked, placing the skull in the center of the bones and bringing a corner of the tarp over.

"Somebody beat me to it." He grinned.

"Where were you?" I asked, bringing the remaining corners over one by one until I had a rectangular-shaped bundle that might have held about anything from buffalo chips to hailstones.

"Around," he said. "Someday maybe I'll tell you something."

As I got to my feet and lifted the bundle he drifted out of the willow patch, and in a moment I heard his pinto trotting upriver.

I'll catch him later and coax it out of him, I thought.

Carrying the bundle to the buckboard, I placed it gently in the back.

Sarah sat with the reins in her hands. Her dark blue eyes rinsed with tears looked blankly out at the debris of life and death.

I looped the steeldust's reins over the saddle horn and then climbed up beside her, took the reins from her slack fingers, and started the team going toward camp.

Steeldusty followed along like a smart cow pony should.

I was glad she hadn't been around when the halfbreed had pointed out the broken leg bone and the gnawed willows, and I asked quietly, "Feeling better?"

"A little." She shook her head tiredly, then set her jaw again like she'd come to another fence to jump and said, "He wasn't even wounded, was he?"

"Not unless a knife got in between his ribs."

"But he was horseback," she said, musing, looking off as she pictured the scene in her mind's eye. "He was fighting rear guard, his horse was plunging from one side to the other as he fired and ran, then turned to fire again . . ." She closed her eyes as she visualized the horse rearing and falling. "Dear God . . ." Her voice dropped to a sorry whisper. "His horse must have fallen . . . that's why his right leg was broken so badly. . . ."

"Steady on, girl," I said, knowing right then that she was a very smart country girl.

Her eyes opened, and she stared at me.

"He crawled in there to hide!" she cried out suddenly. "He couldn't get out even after the Indians had left, but he was alive!"

I wrapped an arm around her, with not a damned helping word to mumble to her.

"General Falls . . ." she said dully. "He left Tommy there, didn't he?"

"Yes, he did. He was over yonder killing a thousand

horses while your brother was trying to hang on over here."

"And they were going to honor him!" she said, as if it were astonishing news. "Honor the cowardly murderer of my brother."

"Yes," I agreed, thinking he could have gone on and become president and Commander-in-Chief if somebody hadn't axed his head off.

"I will bury Tom's bones somewhere else," she said quietly after a moment. "I will not let him be a part of this exhibition."

"It's not over yet."

"You mean the general's circus?" she asked in a bitter voice.

"There's a killer still loose," I murmured, stopping the team near her tent.

"I hope he's never caught," she said strongly.

"Suppose he gets mad at somebody else and settles it in the dark of the night?"

"He won't," she said. "Give it up, Sam. Let him go."

"Reckon I can worry about that after I catch him," I said, stepping down to the ground. "We should put this in a safe place for now." I touched the folded-over tarp.

"It will fit in my hope chest," she said, and she quickly went inside the tent, emerging a minute later lugging a cherrywood chest with dovetailed corners and brass hinges and lock.

There was room left over as I fitted the bundle of bones into the empty chest, but it didn't make any difference. She closed the lid and snapped the lock shut.

"Will you be all right, ma'am?" I asked, taking her hand and looking into the dark blue eyes that had seen more hell in one morning than they'd ever seen in her lifetime.

"I wish I could offer you dinner."

"I'll eat over at camp. Let me know if you need anything."

She squeezed my hand and turned away.

I led the steeldust over to where Skofer and I had laid out our little prairie home, staked him out on some new grass, and walked back up the rise to the main camp, wondering why Skofer was staying out so long.

Young Lieutenant Falls was down at the battle site, where the men were beginning to make a dent in the jumbled bones and trash.

I saw him looking in Minelli's wagon loaded with squared blocks of limestone that had been barred loose from a ledge on the riverbank.

The monument was now above ground a couple of feet. It looked like a stone box with the center filled with dirt. Minelli wasn't wasting any rock that wouldn't show.

I heard Root practicing his speech on over the hill.

"Duty they knew, and duty they did—"

Over at the portable kitchen the fat cook gave me a couple of slices of sourdough bread wrapped around a slab of the leftover buffalo roast.

After that I felt some stronger and wished I had a bottle of brown beer to go with it. Thinking of beer made me think of Skofer, and his beer and nightingale song, and I decided I'd give him another hour before going off looking for him.

I ambled over toward the big daugherty that was originally built to be an ambulance but—like the general's—had been gutted out and rebuilt as a living and working vehicle for his staff.

The open door was on the side and had an iron step.

"Sam Benbow . . . anyone home?" I called from the doorway.

"Come in."

Barr sat humped over a large but portable field desk that would fold up into a wooden case if it had to. Farther along were four bunks, one over the other on each side. On my left was a sturdy narrow table covered with a white sheet, and above it a cabinet holding bottles and small wooden boxes of herbs and drugs that indicated this was the doctor's field hospital.

Opposite that table was a chair and a table stacked with leatherbound books, a sheaf of paper the size of foolscap, a few lead pencils, and a bone-handled penknife.

I figured it to be the great orator's headquarters.

Lieutenant Falls only rated a pine footlocker painted green with his name stenciled on it.

"Come in," Barr said again, looking at me strangely. "Are you all right?"

"Sorry," I said, stepping forward. "I'm gettin' to be as chuckleheaded as a prairie dog with the mumps."

"That's a good one." He smiled, writing a note on a scrap of paper. "I'm trying to collect these western aphorisms."

"If I had a nickel for things like that, my tapeworm wouldn't be hollerin' for fodder."

"Sit down." He wrote that down, too, then coughed into a red neckerchief.

"Got the croup?" I asked, sitting down on the edge of the ladder-back chair.

"Just getting over a touch of grippe that had me down a couple of weeks ago," he said. "What can I do for you?"

"I'm just nosin' around, tryin' to earn that reward."

"You think I killed the old man?" He smiled at me and ran his fingers through his rumpled hair.

"I haven't made my pick yet. You had as much reason as any."

"I don't know anyone who didn't have a reason," he said seriously. "The general's tragedy was that he didn't really have to be such a pure one hundred proof son of a bitch. He could have gotten what he wanted by just letting people like August Root and me get it for him."

"Who would you pick?"

"I'd start with the stonemason, Minelli. He was really fond of the boy."

"Yes, if I were Minelli, I'd have killed him," I agreed. "Who else?"

"Oh, hell, everyone in camp had something against

him. Minelli. Sickle. Snow. Doctor Cadwell. Root.
His son. You. Even Sarah Duffy."

Again he had a coughing attack and pressed the
bandanna against his mouth.

"Better have the doc look at that."

"He's looked at it and prescribes rest and rhubarb
tonic," he said huskily, the red spots on his cheekbones more florid than before.

"That drawing of the general you did last night . . .
you still have it?"

"You heard me tell the lieutenant this morning that
I tore it up," he said, a worried question in his
hound-dog eyes.

"Maybe you spoke a little hasty," I said. "Can I see
the scraps?"

"I could tell you I burned them, but in spite of my
profession I don't lie often." He chuckled and opened
up a stiff buckram portfolio, took out the top page,
and handed it over to me. "I promise you, if I'd killed
the old bastard, I wouldn't show you this."

He'd caught the general perfectly in one of his worse
moments. His sagging head, his short beard, his pig
eyes bulging, his twisted mouth snarling under the
broad, fleshy nose, and he'd added the tusks of a wild
boar to each side of the mouth so that the general
looked more like a charging Russian wild boar than a
human being.

He'd captioned the portrait "Hail to the Chief."

"You have a strange sense of humor," I said,
handing the paper back. "No wonder you didn't want
to send it east with the obituary."

"He was giving me one of his set tongue lashings at the time," he said soberly. "This was a way of weathering the storm, so to speak."

"Getting back at him while he was stompin' you." I nodded. "Pulling a trick on him right under his big nose. How'd you ever learn all this writin' and drawin' stuff?"

"God, Sam, I don't know," he said tiredly. "My father was an actor, a smart man, but couldn't hold still. I went to school and learned my three Rs but never amounted to much until he flew the coop and left Mother and me to make our way. There was an opening as a printer's devil. The writers and artists were good men. They taught me all I could learn."

"And tellin' lies for the general, how'd you get tolled into that?"

"During most of the war he sat at a desk reading newspapers and picking out items that would help move him up the ladder. He liked my style and offered me double my wage just to create the myth of General Frederick Falls. You must admit I did a pretty good job of it."

I nodded and asked, "But do people like Grant and Sherman and Sheridan believe this stuff?"

"It doesn't make any difference once the snowball starts rolling down the hill. When the public has a hero, only a fool would get in the way of it."

"You were goin' to roll that snowball clear into the White House, weren't you?" I murmured.

"That's the truth." Barr nodded. "But that snowball is melting in hell right now."

92

"You don't seem too broken-hearted about it."

"I'm tired," he said slowly. "The general was right, in a way. I've been lagging. I need a rest, but he was a hard driver. There never was time. Right this minute I feel like lying down and sleeping a year and a half."

"No offense, Mr. Barr," I said, "but didn't it kind of bother you to make a silk purse out of a pig's ear?"

He looked at me hard for a second, then spoke softly. "In the city of love in this land of opportunity, a fatherless twelve-year-old boy paid the rent and butcher bill, too, by learning how to lie. . . ."

7

Duty! Duty to serve our destiny. Duty to serve our nation, which will one day shine as a beacon of hope for the world. Duty to our hallowed colors! Say not it is only a flag made of common cotton, say rather it is a sacred and majestic banner waving over the land of the free and the home of the brave . . ."

The whining prairie wind carried Root's practiced oratory around to our camp, where Skofer was picketing his roan and grumbling.

"It's a long gol-darned ride down there, and not a trace of a little toddy anywhere along the way. . . ."

"I always figure if you make it back alive from any journey in this country, you deserve a whole bunch of drinks," I said, poking at our little campfire.

"Where are they?"

He came trotting on his rickety bird legs back into camp like I was all set to uncork a jug.

"I'd guess the nearest drink around here would be in Ellsworth." I smiled. "Unless maybe Doc Cadwell has some medicinal snakebite remedy tucked away in his bag."

"I've caught the chills and fever," he said weakly. "That's what I'm coming down with."

"You're comin' down with a reborn liver and new blood," I said. "Tell me what Mordecai Jones calls hospitality."

"That man is one of them that rolls around on the ground when he prays," Skofer said disgustedly. "He don't drink, smoke, or chew, but he's long on children. He's got a brood of sons just as mean and greedy as he is. They talk about land like it was fire stolen from the gods."

"How many guns can he muster up?"

"I'd say six, if you count the twelve-year-old, and then he's talking about his brethren coming from Pennsylvania to help out."

"He could just as well have laid out his claims north and south instead of east and west," I said, which was true enough, but the river ran east and west, and all the immigrants wanted water even more than land.

Old Mordecai Jones might have six miles of mostly flood plain a quarter mile wide that he couldn't count on growing anything on, but he'd have all the water.

The jayhawkers had already blocked the trail farther on east because they feared the Texas fever, but there were still a couple million longhorns down in Texas to be driven north.

The South Texas Cattlemen's Association couldn't afford to have one lunatic and his brethren control the Western Trail. Maybe in another five or ten years, when the railroads made trail driving look old-fashioned and high-priced, they could fence in the whole Big Pasture and plow deep while others sleep, but right now our cattle had as much right to the range as anything else, including Indians and sod-busters.

Old Mordecai Jones would be going to heaven a little early if he couldn't accommodate our use of the trail we'd blazed long before he got the call to go forth and plow.

"Does he show fight?" I asked Skofer. "I mean, how close is he to buckin' the tiger?"

"Oh, he's up to the tiger's whiskers, ready to stick his head in his mouth right now. I expect they'll all be dead by next week."

"Any sign of a drive comin' close?"

"I knew you'd ask that, and as long as Mordecai Jones didn't smoke, drink, chew, or talk, I used my time riding south down the trail. There's a herd ramrodded by Red Fogarty coming slow."

"Tell Fogarty to hogtie his temper?"

"I told him there was an army of bluecoats over here would take his cows if he wasn't careful when they meet up with Jones."

"Reckon you're spry enough to hoof it down to the battlefield?" I asked, getting to my feet and looking over at the troopers trudging along soldier fashion, slowly moving the unnatural clutter over into the river. "I need to talk to the lieutenant."

"Hell's fire, I only rode fifty miles today!" Skofer shook his head.

"Maybe we ought to saddle up and ride over. That walkin' makes my knees rattle."

"My horse is tired, too," Skofer grumbled. "What is it? About three hundred yards?"

"I'd guess."

"If I keel over, call the doctor and tell him I been bit by a big rattler about twenty times."

"You're dreamin' with your eyes open," I said. "Get some rest while you can."

The lieutenant stood facing the big sergeant of the burial detail, and his young voice was crackling.

"I don't give a good goddamn whether the general said to bury them in a common grave! I'm saying you'll do it the right way and dig a separate grave for each man."

"Yes, sir. That's proper . . . I was just sayin' . . ."

The sergeant was trying to back off when I said, "Lieutenant, there are more."

"More? Where?" He turned and stared at me hard.

"Those missing-in-action troopers of Company A. There's eighteen of 'em about a mile and half downriver."

"You saw them?"

"I counted them." I nodded. "They weren't as scattered as these."

"I thought there were nineteen missing," Lieutenant Falls said slowly, studying my face.

"There were," I nodded. "Miss Duffy intends to bury her brother someplace else."

"For Christ's sake, why?" the lieutenant demanded.

"She figures there's a hoodoo on this place. The sun casts a yellow shadow. Too much wrong and not enough right."

"I guess that's her business." He let out his breath in a long sigh and made a little smile. "We'll have to work by lanterns to finish up before the brass shows up."

"I'd guess if you planted those bones three feet deep instead of six no animal would bother them, and nobody above ground would know the difference."

He thought about it a couple of seconds, nodded, and turned to the sergeant. "Get a wagon and some more gunny sacks and take a detail downriver."

"Yessir." The sergeant saluted and glared at me as he trudged off.

"Were they trapped?" the lieutenant asked in a low voice.

"They were flanked, but some of 'em could have been saved."

"Goddamn it to hell—" He looked at the ground and shook his head. "There's been a general in every generation of my family since the battle of Bunker Hill, but I'm going to break that string just as soon as I finish this up."

"Resign?"

"Right. It's not my idea of living a life that's too darned short to start with."

"But you've always been army. It's different bein' a workin' man."

"I don't suppose it'll be easy," he muttered. "They dressed me in a uniform when I was four years old and gave me a toy musket to carry around. I think it was right then that Father started giving me commands and demanding the correct military response, or I'd get the proper military punishment. Once they put that uniform on me Mother faded away and Father took charge."

"And he knew how to save his skin, butter up the right people, and pass right up the ladder." I nodded.

"But is that reason enough to kill him?" The lieutenant stared at me, his youthful face hardening into a block of dark oak.

"I don't know if folks would murder a man just because they didn't like the way he wore his hat, but there's some that don't mind improvin' the human race."

"I can't think of anyone here that would fit that," the lieutenant said, "except maybe the doctor, and he's sworn to save lives, not take them."

"Can you tell me the straight story on him?" I asked mildly.

"That outburst of my father's"—he flushed—"it was one of his tricks. If he couldn't find anything else to beat a junior officer with, he'd use me for a club. Most people thought I'd just say exactly what he told me to say, and so it never came to a court martial, where I would have told the simple truth no matter what."

"Then the doctor is really completely innocent?"

"I'm not sure." The lieutenant's face flushed again. "But I doubt if any misconduct could ever be proved."

"Are you in on the deal with August Root?" I asked, still fishing.

"I don't even know what it is." He shook his head.

"Somethin' to do with a memorial parkland?"

"It's something to do with taking about ten square miles out of the land reserved for homesteading and saving it for a fort or something." He shook his head. "Father kept quiet about his business deals."

"Ten square miles would make a nice little town site," I murmured, figuring it would take in Mordecai Jones's claims easy enough, and considerable more than that.

"Are you making any progress?" he asked as I turned away.

"I've got to talk to some more people yet," I said. "Is there anyone who can swear you were in your bunk all that night?"

"No, because I wasn't. I was so upset by Father's performance I couldn't sleep," he said quietly. "After an hour or so I got up and checked the sentries."

"Were the other three people asleep in the daugherty when you came back?"

"Yes, I think so. I didn't really look. It was dark and seemed normal enough."

"Hard to eliminate three people who claim they were all asleep in the same room, especially when the fourth one went for a walk."

"Have you talked to Minelli?" the lieutenant asked.

"He's next."

Minelli troweled a soupy mixture of river sand and cement from his wheelbarrow and lifted a limestone slab that crumbled in his big hands and almost fell.

The monument was now about three feet high, and he had kept filling it with dirt as the walls rose.

I dipped my finger in the mortar and rubbed it against my thumb.

"Lots of sand and short on cement," I said to his back.

He set the crumbling rock so that it didn't fall out, then turned to me, his dark face hard and menacing.

"You know more about my business than me?" he challenged.

"I know a short mix when I see it," I said. "And you know that dirt inside will compact in time and leave a hollow space."

"You want me to break my back filling it up with rock?" he demanded. "Why should I? My Johnny ain't buried here."

"I'd think a master mason would just figure on doing a good job."

"Not this time," he growled, slopping more of the mortar onto the rocks. "This time I pay back just what they give me."

"Who are you paying back, Joe?"

"General Frederick Falls, murderer of children," he said over his shoulder. "Called me a goddamned dago, didn't he?"

Minelli turned around with a big smile on his face and winked his right eye at me. "But this goddamned dago is alive, and that fat son of a whore is not sayin' nothin' no more."

"How long do you think your monument will last, Joe?" I asked idly, kneeling and breaking chips off one of the weathered rocks.

"It don't make no difference, does it?" He laughed. "The general said, 'Joe, you dumb dago, put the monument right there.' I tried to tell him that it'll flood up here someday, but no, he says 'Shut up, Joe!' so I shut up."

"The monument won't last?" I asked, wondering if he was right.

"'Course not! First time river rises, say good-bye. It'll sink and fall over."

"So you figure it doesn't make any difference if the rocks are rotten and the mortar short?"

"'At's-a right!" He laughed. "General says put it there, Joe puts it there. Big man knows everything. Dumb dago don't know nothin'."

"The graves?"

"Look at the little wooden crosses." He pointed at the pile of white-painted markers. "Better to use them for firewood and get some good out of them."

"I think you're right, Joe," I said morosely.

Next year or the year after this low, flat ground would be deep in rich grass, and there wouldn't be anything left to mark the spot where six hundred troopers butchered three hundred men, women, and children.

Just as well, I thought.

"Look, Mr. Benbow," Minelli said as he set another rock, "they want the show. They want the speech. They want to feel brave and sad. But just for one day. Then they go somewhere else. Don't bother me no more. I'm glad I put Johnny on the high ground and used a good rock that'll be there a hundred years from now."

"Why were you in camp last night?" I asked casually.

"I could hear the general a mile away in my wagon."

He spit on his big lime-burned hands and hefted another rock to see if it would fit. It wouldn't.

"What did you come for, though? Pilfering?"

"No, I don't steal nothin'. I hope somebody shoot him in the belly."

"I suppose you went back to your wagon and slept sound as a block of Carrera marble all night, too," I said.

"That's right." He chipped at the edge of the rock with a mason's hammer.

"While you were wandering around camp in the shadows, did you happen to see anything or anyone that looked out of place?"

"The general was out of place." He grinned. "Now he's where he should be."

"Did you kill him?"

"I was goin' to," he said carefully, the muscles in his

huge forearms swelling with the effort of lowering the rock gently in place, "but I was goin' to shoot him on the ceremony day right in front of everybody. I was goin' to shoot him first, then I got eight shots left for eight other sonsabitches."

"Didn't you think somebody might start shootin' back?"

"Now it don't make a difference. It's all over. Joe go back to Italy when Joe finish the job."

"Like it better there?"

"I like the people," he said softly. "These people here just want to kill everybody and build monuments."

"Did you steal the plaque?"

"No." He shook his head, rubbing his fingers over the rocks, measuring them and their equilibrium with practiced hands. "It was wrong what that plaque said, and I told the general after he went to bed I wouldn't put it on my monument even if he found it."

"I suppose he was vexed with you."

"He was too drunk to talk. He just said to get the hell out." Minelli shook his head.

"That sort of means you're fairly familiar with the inside of the ambulance, Joe."

Back in camp I found sleepy-eyed Skofer sitting on his bedroll, going through his saddlebags, a pained look on his face.

"I must be getting old," he grumbled. "I've mislaid my silk neckerchief."

"You know where Snow holes up?" I asked as soon as I thought he was awake enough to hear me.

"Snow? The halfbreed scout? Him?"

"Him. He knows something I need to know."

"I saw him come in from upriver yesterday morning. Likely he's found a cave or a hollow log."

"Why wouldn't he sleep out under the stars like everybody else?"

"Because . . . because he's half bear and half badger. That answer your question?" he sputtered testily.

"Sho' now," I said, "reckon we could look him up?"

"I do reckon," he said with a snort. "You sure you haven't got a little bottle of brandy hid out?"

"I'm sure," I said, going for the horses. "Keep your eyes open."

"Open for what?" He sputtered some more.

"Your silk neckerchief."

We rode upriver, working through the scattered timber until Skofer proved himself almost right.

The scout had built a lean-to of poles and brush and spread his buffalo robe inside. In front was a small rock fire ring holding only a few coals. The brown leaves fallen from black walnut trees made a thick carpet, and a length of an ancient cottonwood log that might have floated downstream in the last flood was lodged against two tree trunks. With the coarse bark worn off long ago it made a good enough bench to sit on.

A fresh deer hide was stretched over the end of the log like a drumhead, and hanging from a walnut tree out of any stray animal's reach hung the dressed-out hindquarters of a deer.

As soon as he recognized us Snow sat back on the log and waited silently.

"Howdy," I said, stepping down from the steeldust. "Nice little camp you've got here, Snow."

"They're all the same." He shrugged, not looking at me. "You want meat?"

"No, thanks," I said. "Right now all we want is a little parley."

"I didn't kill him," Snow said, still looking at the ground.

"I haven't asked you that yet." I grinned. "We got to keep things in proper order, you know."

"Everybody has a different order," he said stubbornly. "I didn't kill him or nothin'."

"All right, make a note of that, Skofer." I smiled, and Skofer cocked his head and stared at me.

"What I'm interested in is you, Snow, even if you didn't kill the general."

"I'm nothin'. Born nothin'. Not Indian. *Blanco tampoco.*"

"Still, you're a good scout out in the wilderness, or the general wouldn't have kept you around."

"I know the country some." He nodded, his muddy-colored, pockmarked face unreadable.

"Your mother Indian?" I asked, walking by him and taking a seat on the other end of the log.

"Sure," he nodded.

"Kiowa?"

"Sure," Snow said.

"She dead?" I asked, so he'd know I was going to keep after him until I had it right.

"I could lie," he said. "You wouldn't know."

"Skofer and me are good at this game same as you're good at yours. Just don't waste our time."

"She's dead," he nodded. "She lived in the lower village."

"But you never told the general there was a village down there," I said, beginning to see some sense in the confusion of my mind.

"That's right. He already knew about the big village up this way. He sent in his false peacemakers and promised to come back the next afternoon with gifts and a peace parley, but I didn't say nothin' about the other camp because in that camp was my mother and the rest of my family."

"So that's why the general didn't know there was an armed camp down there when he sent Company A after the runaways?"

"I didn't tell him." Snow shook his head and pursed his lips into a thin line. "But he didn't tell me he was goin' to catch the big village asleep and kill them all. I believed him like everybody else did. I thought he wanted peace."

"You had friends in the upper village?"

"Sure. Some . . . my girl," he murmured. *"Asi es."*

"Plenty good reason to get back at the general," Skofer said.

I pulled the Barlow out of my pants pocket, opened

a blade, and scraped the dirt from under my finger-nails, then found a twig I could whittle on as we talked.

"I didn't kill nobody," he said stolidly.

"You spend last night with anyone?" I asked.

"Me? Hell, nobody but an Indian would spend a night with me, and there ain't no Indians left."

"You said you had somethin' to tell me."

"*Nada.* I did mean to kill him, but somebody else got him first. Maybe I seen him walkin' away in the shadows, but I couldn't see good enough. *¿Quien sabe?*"

"To an expert interrogator, I'd say you're not telling the whole truth," Skofer chuckled.

"I seen him. *Solamente un hombre.*"

"Couldn't have been the woman?"

"Could've been, if she wore pants." Snow smiled slightly.

I finished up with the twig and, while I was looking around for another one, thumped the bone handle of the Barlow on the smooth gray log.

Skofer cocked his head like a jaybird trying to hear an angleworm and said softly, "Do that again."

"Do what again?" I reached for a twig suitable for whittling.

"Thump that log again."

I thumped it again, nodded at Skofer, and said quietly, "Snow, if you make a move to run, I'll shoot your buckskins off."

"Why would I run?" He frowned. I noticed a greasy sweat glistening on his fat face. "*¿Porque?*"

"Take a look, Skofe."

Not waiting, he'd already pulled the raw deer hide off the end of the log and reached inside.

"Tellin' me I don't know nothing about scouts and hollow logs!" he crowed. "By ye bulls of Bashan, I've never been proved wrong yet!"

Out came a large buckskin-wrapped package, and I said to Snow, "Mind if I look?"

"I can't say no," he said with a shrug.

Skofer unfolded the buckskin and lifted out the bronze plaque, a small velvet-lined case that held three of Doctor Cadwell's scalpels, the lieutenant's bootjack, Root's cuff links, Gerald Barr's pen and ink case, a large, lace-trimmed unmentionable that had to belong to Sarah, and Skofer's silk neckerchief.

"Nothin' of mine in there?" I asked Skofer.

"I guess you ain't got nothing a pack rat wants," Skofer cackled.

"Tell me," I said to Snow.

"I don't take things that cost much. I just like to fool people."

"You look through this stuff every once in a while and laugh yourself silly, I suppose."

"I ain't as dumb as I look."

"Damn it, I don't think you're dumb!" I said angrily. "I always figured bein' on your home ground gave you a head start over the rest of us."

"Maybe that's why I don't have nothin' of yours," he said calmly.

"By golly, Snow, you just overspoke yourself," I

said, looking over at Skofer. "There's nothin' of mine, and . . ."

Skofer squinted his eyes and read my mind. "And there's nothing of the general's."

"And we know what you thought of him." I nodded at Snow.

"There has to be more." Skofer leaned down and reached far back inside the log.

"Eureka!" He grinned and dragged out another bundle.

Snow stood tense as a strung bow. I lifted my Colt from its holster and said, "You're not leavin' just yet."

Skofer opened the bundle in front of us, revealing the bronze peace medal and the otter-bone breastplate on top of the carefully folded war bonnet of Wide Bear.

"Explain," I said.

"They're sacred *santos,*" he said in a very quiet voice. "I was goin' to put them back in Wide Bear's burial tree."

"Very noble of you," Skofer said, folding the buckskin back over the relics again, "but these things were taken the night the general was killed."

"Like I told you . . ." Snow opened his hands to show the futility of explaining. "I went in the general's place that night."

"And you hacked off his head with Wide Bear's axe, too, didn't you?" Skofer asked sharply.

"No." Snow shook his head. "He was already dead. I meant to kill him, all right, why not? I would like to kill all of you."

8

SOLDIERS AND STATESMEN IN THE AUDIENCE TODAY HAVE always been in the vanguard in settling the Indian question, and each of them has learned by hard experience and sacrifice that there is not an Indian alive who can be trusted, that Indians have committed enough dastardly depredations upon innocent white settlers to reap the whirlwind . . ."

Still memorizing his ringing lines and practicing the rise and fall of voice, contrived pauses and rhetorical questions, dramatic gestures and changes in posture, the golden-tongued lion of the prairie practiced his speech for the lamenting north wind.

I wondered, as we brought Snow into camp, if an orator ever did anything except collect his fee. Did he ever cut wood, build a bridge, train a horse, or use his hands for something besides chopping the air with his gestures? I wondered if an orator could ever chop a man's head off with a razor-edged battle axe.

Except for the fancy bosom binder that I'd put into an old sugar sack, and the plaque that I'd held back, all of the pilfered articles were in the buckskin pack that I spread out on the big mess table.

The lieutenant took a look and exclaimed, "Why, that's my bootjack! Where did you find it?"

"Snow," I said, nodding at the halfbreed.

The others came over to the table and picked out their belongings.

"I've been wondering whatever happened to these scalpels," Doc Cadwell said, checking through the leather-covered case. "They're English. Why did you take them, Snow?"

Snow looked stolidly at him, forcing a hangdog smile, and said, "A game I play."

Gerald Barr picked up his writing case from the buckskin, stared at Snow, and said, "You?"

Snow nodded slightly, and Barr started to cough. Huddling his shoulders and bowing his head, he jammed a clean handkerchief to his mouth until the racking cough let up, and he wheezed, "Doctor, can I see you in the infirmary?"

"Certainly," Cadwell said, and the pair moved off toward the daugherty as Sarah Duffy approached and read the scene immediately.

"Snow's been going through our bags?" She looked up at me.

"Yes'm," I said, taking the sugar sack out from under my arm and giving it to her. "I believe this might belong to you."

She blushed a fiery red and murmured, "Thank you, Mr. Benbow."

Before she could say any more, the lion of the prairie came forward with his chest out and back straight, his long hair blowing in the wind, and glared at Snow. "You son of miscegnation, those cuff links were a gift from my stepmother!"

Snow didn't even bother to nod or shrug his shoulders or blink. He either held the politician in complete contempt or had no understanding whatever of what kind of a critter he was.

Skofer set the next buckskin-wrapped packet on the table and opened it up to show the relics of Wide Bear.

"I don't know who these really belong to, maybe no one," he said.

"They belong in Wide Bear's burial scaffold," I said, "but I suppose they'll end up in a museum."

"But they were in Father's ambulance—" The lieutenant read the implication immediately and stared in surprise at Snow. "I thought you were . . ." He started to say 'a friend' but saw how foolish that was before it came out, and he replaced it with "on our side."

"I'm nobody, but I didn't kill him." Snow spoke for the first time.

The doctor came back from the daugherty and caught the tail end of Snow's reply.

"But you could have," he said mildly. "There's the evidence."

"He was already dead," Snow said.

"What a lying rascal he is," Root blared out triumphantly. "Of course he killed the general. The general no doubt discovered his duplicity and would have had him hanged in dawn's early light had not this wretched scoundrel stopped that mighty heart—"

"But no one actually saw him," Sarah said quietly.

Gerald Barr drifted back over to the group, his face paper white, the red roses on his cheeks blooming.

"Did you do it?" Barr asked Snow directly.

"No. Everybody knows I wouldn't do that. You, too."

Barr said nothing but stared into the breed's cloudy eyes and nodded.

"It's simple," Root broke in. "The general caught him in his compartment stealing those trophies. The general grappled with him, and the savage grabbed up the first weapon at hand and dealt him a fatal blow."

"There wasn't any sign of grappling," I said.

"Then as soon as the general opened his eyes and saw it was the halfbreed, he was doomed," Root said vehemently, smacking his right fist into the palm of his left hand. "I say hang the rotten red devil right now!"

"What's the hurry?" I asked. "He ought to have a trial at least."

"What do you say, Doctor?" Root demanded.

"He certainly *looks* guilty enough, but . . ." Cadwell hesitated.

"What about you, Barr?" the lion of the prairie interrupted.

"I'd vote to turn him loose," Barr said, "even if he did it."

"There must be rule by law if we are to remain civilized," Root intoned dramatically. "Justice must be done even unto every fallen sparrow!"

"Justice was done. It's over," Barr said weakly, dabbing at his mouth with the neckerchief.

"Just a minute, all of you," Lieutenant Falls broke in, "we're not going to hang anybody. Our job is to set the stage for the ceremony, and that's enough to keep us all busy."

"What are you going to do? Turn the murderer of your father loose?" Root's round face reddened, and his bloodshot eyes bulged out in anger.

"No. I'm going to have him locked up in the spare ambulance until General Sheridan comes, then turn the whole thing over to him."

"I believe General Sheridan will not be irresolute as some of his junior officers." Root smiled. "I accept the compromise."

Big Sergeant Price and Corporal Mulholland led the uncomplaining prisoner away, and I said to Sarah, "I think I know how you would have voted."

"I would have trouble hanging even the devil for murdering the man who betrayed my brother," she said softly. "What do you think?"

"For Snow, I'd say it's about a fifty-fifty chance he did it," I said. "I could say the same thing about most everyone else, including the lieutenant."

"But surely not Dr. Cadwell?" She frowned and looked at Skofer.

"His whole career would have been ruined if the general had lived." Skofer nodded.

"I'm mixed up," she said as she shook her head. "Losing Tom, to me, is like losing my faith."

"I lost mine in the war," Skofer said. "There was no way I could ever make a prayer to a merciful God over the stacks of dead boys buried in a common pit, but I never quite lost the idea that man is good when man is free."

"Free from what?"

"Free from ignorance, lies, superstition, cant, from all kinds of rulers elected or otherwise." Skofer said like a drinking man who hasn't had a drink for a week. "If he's free, he's really himself."

"You folks goin' to philosophize all day, maybe we can philosophize on figurin' out who killed the general," I put in.

"I'd take a second look at Root," Skofer said. "There's something going on underneath all the horse feathers."

"What do you think, Sarah?"

"I don't want to guess, but the stonemason seems to have so much anger inside, he's capable of anything. Do you have any more evidence?"

"The evidence is right under our noses, but we can't see it," I said. "I haven't talked to Root yet."

"What do you make of that cowboy foggin' it this way?" Skofer asked, squinting off toward the east.

"You said that herd was goin' slow," I muttered,

116

figuring the only place that cowboy could be from was a herd of cattle.

He rode Texas-style tall. His stirrups were armored with tapaderos to keep the Uvalde mesquite from knocking his boots loose, and he wore a big hat the color of dirt.

"Maybe they had a stampede. Maybe they need some help," Skofer muttered hopefully.

The guard passed the cowboy on and pointed at us on the rise, and the rider pushed the sorrel pony on without slowing down.

Skofer and I walked partway down the rise to meet him, and when I saw the Texas rig and the cloverleaf brand on the horse's left hip I knew his herd, and I knew who was ramrodding that herd, too.

"You Benbow?" he asked in a familiar south Texas drawl.

"That's me."

"Boss says you're needed at the ford," he said, his young, sun-blackened face expressionless, his wide eyes hidden under the big pulled-down hat.

"Fogarty in a hurry?" I asked.

"He said 'right now,'" the young Texan said.

I looked at Skofer and said, "Better you stay here and keep an eye out."

"I'm supposed to side you," he protested.

"I need you here," I said, and I went over behind the wagons to the steeldust, tightened the leathers on my saddle, and swung aboard. Riding back to Skofer, I said, "Keep an eye on Minelli, and watch your back."

"Same to you," he said stoutly.

"You don't have to ruin that good pony," I said to the cowboy. "Give him a drink and take your time. I'll find my way."

Pressuring the steeldust's ribs with my knees, I thought I heard Sarah call out, "You be careful!" but the steeldust liked to step right out, and we were already a hundred yards down the slope.

With the steeldust the hardest thing is to hold him down to a reasonable speed. He was bred to run a quarter-mile sprint and catch a longhorn before it knew it was being caught, but even if he could never hold that speed very long, he'd kill himself trying.

I finally got him settled down to a mile-eating easy canter and had time to think about Red Fogarty and his Clover Leaf Ranch down south.

I'd met him a couple times in the San Antonio stockyards and recognized him as a quiet-spoken cattleman who'd been made as hard and lean as mesquite thorns by the dry-fanged range he called home. He was also known as a man with a quick and violent temper when crossed, so folks made a point of never putting a burr under his saddle. He was a lonely man because of it, his only company being the men he hired, and even they didn't last very long.

Mixing Red Fogarty with Mordecai Jones was about like dumping a keg of black powder on a campfire.

So I figured if he said "right now," he wasn't apt to wait very long. Maybe the best thing was that Skofer had already told him if there was killing, he'd be putting his drive in jeopardy because the federal troops might step in.

There wasn't any doubt in any Texan's mind that the soldiers in blue were not even allies. They were the soldiers of oppression supporting the carpetbaggers who were still plundering what little was left of old Texas.

The river moved along in such a long meander it seemed to be straight as a compass line, but by keeping track of the sun I could tell it was really bending a little south.

I thought that whoever named that poor little innocent stream couldn't have guessed just how putrid it would be once the army finished dumping its battle trash into it.

I saw the shed roof of a soddy dugout on the river bank and noticed the land had changed so that the river could spread out more. The banks were broken to gentle inclines by cattle drovers who preferred the solid shallows where they knew there was no bogging quicksand.

From the half dugout, half soddy, Jones had tried to put a rail fence on the southern bank. It was such a flimsy, rickety affair, no Texas longhorn would ever take it as a serious barrier, and I doubted if Red Fogarty would either.

I turned the steeldust and crossed the river toward Jones's soddy dugout.

From the river I could see others on down, poking up like little windowless boxes, their roofs covered with sod laid on cottonwood logs.

There were a couple of wagons, a mechanical haymower parked at random, and a corral that held a few milk cows and mules together. Toward the trees a copper boiler sat on some rocks over a fire, and a shapeless woman bent over it washing clothes.

From the cloud of dust I judged the herd was about a mile down the trail. Fogarty must've hurried them up as soon as Skofer left him.

In the south wall of the soddy were rifle ports, and a rifle barrel shone in one of them.

On ahead three men stood side by side. The young one on the left carried a stick with a white rag tied to it. The middle man with the goose gun I recognized as Mordecai Jones, and the one on his right looked like it might be another young son. They all wore faded union blue, brogans, and soft, drooping wool hats.

They faced three mounted riders coated with dust, no doubt tired and irritable and anxious to get on to Ellsworth. At the front was tall, level-shouldered Red Fogarty riding a short-coupled buckskin gelding.

It looked like one of those pageant plays where the embattled poor folks are defending their home from the wicked robber barons. Maybe that was the scene in Mordecai Jones's mind, and he'd staged it to look that way, but I knew he'd only arrived a couple months before and had been raising more hell than building a home. I knew the Texans' side because I'd done my share of popping brush after the toughest, meanest animals in the world.

I made myself remember the commander's orders: "Don't let anybody provoke a fight and give us a bad name."

Fine, Commander, but suppose the homesteaders

provoke the fight? Suppose they think they're fortified enough that they can stop a herd of longhorns from crossing over?

Red Fogarty saw me coming and said something so that Mordecai and his two grown sons turned to look.

"Howdy, Benbow," Red said through dry lips, his eyes blazing, but with his temper still under control. "Mind tellin' these shit kickers to get out of the way? I wouldn't bother you except for your pardner tellin' me the war is still goin' on."

"Everybody settle down," I said, pulling up the steeldust in the space between the homesteaders and the cowboys.

"Listen to him, Dad," one of the sons warned. "He talks just like cowboys."

"Mr. Jones," I said, "these men want to pass over the river without any trouble."

"Takin' down my fence would be some trouble, I'd say," replied Mordecai Jones, his blocky, bearded face set, his eyes strange.

Just how crazy was he? How far would he go to stop the cattlemen?

"My cows'll take out that little tumbleweed fence and welcome the back scratchin'," Red Fogarty said.

"Don't forget the army's just up the river," Jones said. "I fought with the First Pennsylvania, myself."

"I ain't got all day, Benbow," Red Fogarty growled.

"Red, there's a ford downriver a couple of miles."

"Boggy?"

"I don't really know," I said, "but it'd be better'n startin' a ruckus here."

"You're supposed to be workin' for the cattlemen, Benbow," Fogarty rasped out.

"My boss told me plain out we don't want any bloodshed just now."

"Your boss is settin' on his fat rump in an easy chair down in Austin," Red said bitterly. "Now I tell you, I ain't goin' to put up with this much more'n about a minute longer."

Trying to keep the spark from lighting, I turned to Jones and said, "The Cattlemen's Association will pay for your damages. Just get out of the way so nobody gets hurt."

"This is my ground," Jones said stubbornly. "Me and my sons own six miles of riverbank. You folks have to go east or west, because we ain't movin'."

"The cattle are here, though," I said. "Better to compromise some and let them cross peaceable."

"If we let you go by, there'll just be somebody else comin' along wantin' the same privilege."

"Privilege!" Red snapped with angry disgust.

He'd had the privilege of sun and dust and alkali, hostile, hungry Indians and renegade rustlers snapping their blankets in the night amongst the herd, dug out and drug bogged-down cows from the quicksands, endured hailstorms and the constant prairie wind, lost good horses to prairie dog holes and cutbanks in the night, all on a diet of beef, beans, and biscuit and in one set of clothes.

Now it was a privilege to cross a God-given river.

"The hell with it, Benbow," Red said hotly. "They're too damned lint-headed to listen to your terms, and I'm too damned tired to go lookin' for another ford. Get out of my way!"

"Red, you're being' just as lint-headed as these hayseeds here." I tried to grin and kid him out of it, but he was much like his longhorns; he could never get over bein' mad.

"You for me or against me?" he asked, his hand drifting toward the butt of his six-gun.

"Red, hold on. I give up gunfightin'. Let's be reasonable."

"I ain't reasonable. Nobody ever lived very long in Texas is reasonable. You been out in the world too much, Benbow, sidin' with pukes. Now, goddamn you, back up or make your play!"

The punchers alongside him moved apart, giving him plenty of room. I eased back on the reins with my left hand and set my boots forward to make the steeldust back up.

Red had lost what little sense he had by then and maybe thought I was doing something besides what he'd just told me to do—back up. I was practically sitting on the steeldust's tail, I wanted to back up so much, but horses don't back up fast. It's not a natural gift for them, and Red, if he'd thought about it, knew it as well as I did. But no, he'd forgot all about everything he'd ever learned except to shoot the hell out of whatever was pesterin' him.

The steeldust, with his neck arched and his jaw tucked in prettily, made one back step and started the other, and Red spiked his right hand down, gripped the walnut butt, and brought up the heavy Colt.

I had him beat by a quarter of a second and tried a shot at his right side, hoping to hit his gun or his arm.

Was a good enough idea, if it'd worked, but the steeldust still had it in his head to back up, and the awkward movement jogged my aim at the same time Red's buckskin shied so that Red's left side was there when my Colt fired.

Smashing through his left rib cage at heart level, the bullet drove him out of his stirrups, and I couldn't have done worse if I'd tried.

Time later for grieving; right now was Benbow living time, and I swung the Colt to cover the other drovers.

No one had made a move yet for his gun, and I said, "Don't do nothin' dumb until you think about it."

I guess that was pretty dumb all by itself, but the pair understood what I meant and sat still.

Still holding the six-gun ready in a red, crazy rage, I dismounted and charged the three nesters.

They'd been staring dumbfounded at the dead cattleman and weren't expecting more trouble. I coldcocked the two young ones so goddamned fast they never knew what hit their damn fool farmer's hats. Still swinging, I brought my gun barrel down on Mordecai's wrist, gladly hearing the bone snap.

As his goose gun dropped to the ground I hit him in the jaw with the same gun barrel, then jabbed it in his left eye and pushed as hard as I could. He fell back screaming, but I stayed with him, lifted him up by his blue flannel collar, and kicked him in the balls. He screamed again, and I hit him across the mouth with the gun barrel, breaking off his front teeth, making a red, wet smear of his bearded lips.

He started to fall again, but I held him up with my left hand, jabbed the Colt into his gaunt belly, and asked, "Have I got your attention?"

I was still out of control, but the red burning fog in front of my eyes was splitting into purple blobs, and when he nodded, his one open eye rolling upward, I gritted out, "You are goin' to tear that fence down. If you ever put it up again, I will come back. Do you believe me?"

He nodded again, his left eye squinched shut and leaking serum, his right eye rolling.

"Your women can sell punkin pie and sauerkraut to the cowboys crossin' the river, but you are never goin' to bother them again. You understand that?"

He blatted out an insane moan of terror and pain, and I let him fall to the ground.

The oldest son was half conscious by then, and I threw his musket aside, then kicked him in the ribs. "Did you hear?"

"Yes, sir," the young man yelled, trying to crawl away on his back.

As the two young ones helped Mordecai limp away I simmered down and walked over to where the punchers were standing around Red Fogarty's body. I'd known in the essential instant where my bullet had gone, and it was just plain hopeless he could be any other way than dead.

"Who's segundo?" I asked quietly.

"I reckon it's me," a short, wide-barreled, wrinkle-faced puncher said, facing me.

"I'm sorry," I said, half sick. "I was tryin' for his arm."

"He pushed it, mister," the segundo said. "He pushed once too often. Still and all, he was a Texas cowman—"

"When you're ready, take your herd on over," I said.

I mounted up the steeldust and rode back toward the river. Half a dozen ragged-ass Joneses were tearing down the fence rails as I passed on by. From the soddy I heard Mordecai scream as someone tried to fix his eye or his teeth. I hoped I'd ruptured his balls and cut off his meachy seed.

— 9 —

I FELT A THOUSAND YEARS OLD AT DAYBREAK WHEN AN
overbearing polecat of a bugler blew reveille and
about that time somebody else started caterwauling
like he'd banged his head on a hornet's nest.

What it was, it was somebody else's business, I
thought drowsily, looking over to see that Skofer was
already up and gone.

I'd slept a few minutes overtime, but it wasn't
enough.

I thought about Red Fogarty, sourly picturing the
hothead insisting on his own oblivion, and I thought
I'd killed an honest cattleman because a fool bunch
of nesters wouldn't get out of the way. That wouldn't
set well back down in Texas. With any luck the
commander'd fire me.

But if I could figure out who'd chopped the general's

head off, I could tell the commander that it was too late to fire anybody because Skofer and I were hightailin' it to California.

They had the halfbreed locked up, but I didn't think there was enough evidence to hang him. Need something a little extra to bulldog the reward money. Likely it wasn't him anyway. At the moment I didn't give a damn. I'd have hung any of 'em for a thousand dollars, including the general's son.

But I was feeling a little scratchy just then, groaning to myself as I dragged my boots on.

The caterwauling over the rise faded away by the time I was set to face the day with a cup of burned boot juice the mess cook called coffee.

"Goddamn it to hell," I grumbled to no one.

Skofer arrived as if I'd just called him by name, his lined, rosy cheeks looking like last year's McIntosh apples, but his eyes were dead serious.

"He broke out," he announced sadly, like I should follow with the Lord's Prayer.

"What the hell you talkin' about?" I growled, trying the coffee again. The cup was hot and the coffee cold.

"Snow."

I was about to bite his head off for talking about snow when I remembered it was the breed's name.

"There goes our trip to California," he said mournfully.

"It wasn't him that did it," I said, mixing in half a cup from the pot to see if I couldn't get it somewhere near warm.

"Who did?"

"We got another problem," I said grumpily, and I told him about Red Fogarty and a little about Mordecai Jones.

"Commander'll catch holy hell for it," Skofer said, "and he'll pass it right on to us with a red-hot pitchfork."

"I took the chance that Red wasn't altogether on a hair trigger," I said, "and we both lost."

"It's over and done with," Skofer said encouragingly. "Maybe it'll be a month or so before we see the commander, and by then he'll be mad about something else."

"Skofer, listen close. I'm sick of killin' people. I got killin' stuck in my craw, and I got to get it out or it'll choke me down."

"Mercy, let's head west then," he said mildly.

"You think that killin' shadow won't follow along?"

"Not if we're just normal citizens working a shift in a mine or selling tack hammers in a hardware store, or maybe you'd like to keep busy weighing up little bags of red beans—"

"I don't know why I waste my time on you," I growled, wondering why it had to be that way . . . killin' on one side, monotony on the other.

I wrapped a leftover flapjack around some cold bacon and called it breakfast, downed another cup of the thick black road-building material, and decided I was ready to meet the day if the day was ready to meet me.

"What the hell happened to Snow?" I asked.

"I was wondering if you'd lost interest," Skofer said. "He flew the coop."

"Let's look," I said, walking on over toward the spare ambulance parked near Company B's tents.

"They didn't post a night guard," Skofer said. "Figured he couldn't get at the lock on the outside of the door."

"Reasonable," I muttered. "That's what all the yellin' was about?"

"There was some excitement, all right, when the morning guard showed up and found the door open."

No one was watching the ambulance now. They'd barred the door on the outside and left it empty.

"Was it barred like that last night?" I asked Skofer.

"There's no other way to lock it," he replied.

"Then it's easy enough to guess somebody let him out. He'd need arms about nine feet long to reach out through the window and fumble on around the corner to lift that bar."

"Makes sense," Skofer said. "I guess everybody's figured that out by now."

Unbarring the door, I climbed inside. There were benches running along either side for wounded men, and more could be added if needed.

"Nothing. A big goose egg," I said.

"You don't sound too tore up about it," Skofer said reproachfully.

"Somebody let him out."

"Who?" Skofer asked pointedly.

"Whoever killed the general," I said, and I headed back to the camp.

"You're guessing."

"I'll make another guess that he's dead, too," I said.

"How can you figure all that out when there ain't nothing at all there to figure from?"

"He knew who killed the general," I said. "He almost told me down at the lower village, but then he figured to make it pay. Somehow he got the word to that person and figured he'd not only get loose, he'd ride off with a bunch of double eagles in his poke."

"So you figure the gent that murdered the general come up here, let him out, and paid him off?"

"I think we ought to look for his body," I said. "Unless he was dumped in the river."

"What are we doin' up here, then?" Skofer said, short of breath from the uphill walk.

"We're lookin' for the lieutenant. Maybe he can organize a search party."

"He's down at the monument," Skofer said. "Most of his men are cleaning up the lower village."

I looked down at the flat, low land nearly back to normal, leaving only the open graves behind the monument that was now about five feet high.

Dr. Cadwell came out of the daugherty and wandered over our way, his head down a little, as if he had some weighty thing on his mind.

"Mornin', Doctor," I said. "Problem?"

He blinked, straightened up, and murmured, "It's Gerald Barr. He's quite ill."

131

"In bed?" Skofer asked.

He nodded.

"TB?" I asked.

"I'm not at liberty to talk about my patients." He shook his head. "What's so interesting down below?"

I looked back and saw that the lieutenant and Minelli were both staring down into the first grave. Then the lieutenant stepped back and yelled, "Sergeant!"

"Best we look," I said, and we headed down the slope.

By the time I reached the grave the lieutenant and Minelli had clambered down the steep sides. A man lay facedown on a heap of bones.

Muddy-colored skin, and a lot of it, because his buckskin shirt was gone.

The ends of an iron wire noose protruded from the fat back of the neck.

"Ain't you the smart one, though." Skofer muttered in my ear.

"Where's his blouse?" I asked.

"Not here," Lieutenant Falls answered shortly.

The doctor gingerly slid down and knelt over the breed named Snow.

"Simple strangulation," he said. "Rigor mortis has set in, so he's been dead more than four hours."

"You might as well wrap him in a blanket and leave him there," I said.

"No." The lieutenant shook his head and lifted his hand up for me to grab. "He won't lie with these men."

". . . Now is that solemn moment as we prepare to take leave of our honored brothers elected by the Divine Will to the Valhalla of all American soldiers who gave their lives that this nation might grow and prosper . . ."

The reedy voice of the lion of the prairie swelled and diminished in volume as the wind brought snatches of his speech down the slope.

"He's about got it down letter perfect," I said.

"I'd rather listen to just the wind," the lieutenant said, and he leaned down to help the doctor out of the pit.

"About time that poor man had a rest," I said, nodding toward Root's stubby figure off to the side of the rise, a sheaf of paper in his left hand, waving like a stork's wing.

"Need any help?" Skofe asked.

"The elder's advice is always welcome." I grinned at the rickety little rooster.

"The elder's first advice is to honor thy elder by praising him," Skofer cackled.

By the time we reached August Root he was studying a new page and mouthing the words silently.

The wind keened over the dry prairie grass and ruffled his silky mane.

"You write all that yourself, Mr. Root?" I asked, coming up behind him.

He jumped about four inches and whirled around like he was expecting a wild Injun. When he saw me and Skofer he frowned and snapped, "Next time, please announce yourselves ahead of time."

"I was askin' if you wrote it yourself."

"The eulogy? Almost all of it. I had some help from Gerald Barr, of course."

"How's he feelin'?" I asked.

"Taken a turn for the worse, I'm afraid. I hope it's nothing more than the grippe."

"You close to him?" I asked.

"We have both been associated in General Falls's business for several years," he said, glancing at me suspiciously. "Why?"

"Just curious. I hear somebody say you were from Baltimore?"

"No. I was born and raised in a little town called Blackwater, in Pennsylvania, and if you think I would murder my partner, you're crazy," he snapped angrily.

"Partner?" Skofer asked, keeping him off balance.

"Silent partner, then. General Falls and I control a corporation that has various assets and interests. He had a most astute mind for business."

"Little hard to get along with sometimes," I observed. "Like the roasting he gave you the night he was killed—called you a little monkey. Hard to swallow that."

"After a few times, you get used to it. General Falls had a bitter tongue, it's true, but he made things happen that lesser men could not do."

"You mean in your corporation?" I asked.

"Yes. And in his career, and in his service to the people of America."

"You grew up in Blackwater?" I asked.

"Eleven years," he said, his thin, foxy mouth twisted. "My father was a coal miner. He put me in the pit with a pick and shovel when I was eleven years old to help support the family."

"Big family, I suppose."

"There were nine of us that lived," he grated. "Nobody could dig enough coal to support that brood and better himself at the same time."

"You'd have ended up just like your dad, with a batch of kids and wore out . . ." Skofer said.

"That's true." Root nodded thoughtfully. "But—once I figured out that the man buying the coal had the money and the man digging the coal didn't, I left."

"You run off?"

"It's hard to believe, but I got as far as Boston before I fainted from hunger." He nodded. "You see, I had the notion that to get ahead you had to mix in with the rich."

"But you fainted from hunger," Skofer reminded him.

"Yes, but I did it in the richest neighborhood in the city." He grinned wisely.

"You were an awfully bright child," Skofer said admiringly.

"I woke up in the biggest, fanciest kitchen I'd ever seen. A black servant was trying to spoon some soup into me, and a gray-haired lady in satin and rubies was watching.

"To make a long story short, she and her husband

were childless. They hired a special tutor so that I could make up for lost time and finally enter Harvard."

"Beat the coal pit all to pieces," Skofer said agreeably.

"It's still in the back of my mind," Root said, "and so is my black-faced father, coming in the front door so tired he could hardly make it to a chair."

"Then you went into government work, I suppose?" Skofer asked.

"When the war started, the government grew by leaps and bounds. At the age of thirty, I am the youngest Assistant Secretary of War in the history of our country," Root said proudly.

"Think it'll change much with the general dead?"

"Not much." He shook his leonine head. "There's always another general willing to capitalize on his position."

"You mean make more money?" I asked.

"Capitalize is what I said." He grinned that foxy way again, his eyes squinched up like he was admiring his own shrewdness.

"I'm wonderin' how you mean to handle this memorial land preserve," I said mildly. I didn't expect an honest answer, but he surprised me by his counter.

"Yes, I had a report that you killed a cattleman down at the ford yesterday. I've been meaning to offer my congratulations."

"It wasn't exactly my doin'," I said, on the defensive. I didn't want to talk or think about it.

"You roughed up Jones, too, I heard," he said, eyeing me closely.

"Every twenty years I lose my temper," I murmured.

"It doesn't really matter. Jones will be leaving soon. He was just doing his job."

"Job?" Skofer asked, putting his hand to his ear like he was hard of hearing.

"Jones was employed to occupy that stretch of land until September fifth, when it will pass into the hands of the Blackwater Land Preservation Corporation," Root said carelessly, looking beyond us, tired of our small talk.

"You mean he was just there to keep other homesteaders out?" I nodded, like I knew it all. "Sort of reservin' for the preservin'."

"Very good!" he chuckled. "I wish the general could have heard that."

"What about the western trail for the cattlemen?" Skofer asked.

"They're welcome to use it until a city is built. By then, though, the railroad will be through here and on west to Santa Fe, and they won't even need it," he said. "Now, if you don't mind . . ."

"I'm kind of wonderin' about Jones," I said. "It seems to me he showed a lot of fight for ground he didn't even own."

"He showed fight for the money he was promised, that's all," Root said. "If he wasn't convincing, he wouldn't be paid."

"Kind of like the coal miner," Skofer said. "If you don't dig coal, you don't get your groceries."

"You understand it perfectly," Root said with a fake smile.

"But then how are you goin' to transfer all this land to your private corporation?" I asked.

"I'm not saying any more about the corporation's plans, but I assure you it will all be legal and proper."

"I suppose if the general had lived, you were figuring on picking up a few pieces of the Dakota territory, too."

"You'll just have to wait and see." Root flashed a sharp-toothed smile at me and patted the rolled-up sheaves of paper in the palm of his left hand, waiting for us to go away like good little boys.

"Is General Sheridan in your corporation, too?" I asked.

"I really can't say, Mr. Benbow. If you'll excuse me . . ."

"Sherman?"

"Mr. Benbow, please."

"Grant?"

"You're entirely out of order, gentlemen," he said sharply. "Now please leave."

"Hell's fire, Root," I muttered, "I killed a good cowman yesterday because I believed I was in the right, but now you're tellin' me it was just a show for ignorant galoots. I'm some vexed about that."

"All right," he said, his face flushing red, "you believed the show, but that's because you were supposed to. It wasn't your fault that it was a very good show."

"Who are these Jones folks really?" Skofer asked.

"I found them in the Blackwater pit with not a prayer for improving their lot. Believe me, they were overjoyed when I offered them the chance to go west."

Before I could twist the lion's tail some more, Sarah Duffy came out of her tent, carrying a flour sack full of clothes, and her path to the river came close enough for Root to speak up.

"Good morning, Miss Duffy, may I be of any help to you?"

"No, thank you," she replied politely. "I'm just going to do some washing."

After she'd passed on by, Root made a fist and kissed the hole between his thumb and forefinger with a loud smack, then he glanced at me with a studdy man-to-man leer and murmured, "I wonder what she'd charge for that."

Even with Skofer hanging onto my arm and screeching under his breath, I still managed to knock Mr. August Hamilton Root senseless with just one overhand right.

10

FROM THE STAFF TABLE SKOFER AND I COULD SEE THE burial detail bringing the remains of Company A troopers to the new cemetery. Lieutenant Falls and his big sergeant stood by as a wagonload of full gunny sacks pulled up.

Minelli's monument appeared to be a square field-stone block with the beginnings of a pyramid on top. He'd built a rough scaffold to work on the top section.

Sarah Duffy sat beside me and looked down at the distant scene.

"It's almost over except for the covering up," she murmured.

"They still have to put up the crosses with the names on them."

"All just sham to make everyone feel warm and cozy inside," she observed without bitterness.

Gerald Barr and Dr. Cadwell came over from the daugherty and sat across from us. The doctor seemed to be in a serious mood, and Barr, though his long, angular face was still pale and the splotches of red on his thin cheeks more defined, seemed to be extra cheerful.

"You're lookin' better," I said to him.

"Right as rain." He smiled wryly. "I've always had a weak chest. The doctor says I've been on the verge of galloping pneumonia, but the worst of it's over."

"It's partly due to the emotional strain of the past few days," the doctor said.

August Root, the lion of the prairie, came over and took a stool at the end of the table, as far away from me as he could get. The knot on the side of his face made him look like a bulldog with lumbago.

"What strain?" he asked gruffly.

"Losing the boy, then the general . . ." Dr. Cadwell said. "One's resistance to disease goes down at such times."

"Ah, well," Root said with a smile, "the general is sleeping peacefully, free from this vale of tears, pain, and woe."

"I hope he's roasting in hell," Sarah Duffy said quietly.

"Judge not lest ye be judged," Root reproached her. "When do we eat?"

"Soon as the lieutenant comes, sir," the black mess cook said from over by the fire.

"I'm so hungry I could eat half a buffalo." Gerald Barr grinned crookedly. "I missed my breakfast."

"I want you to go slow for a couple more days," the doctor cautioned.

I thought the doc's haggard face looked worse than Barr's.

"Tomorrow it'll all be over," Barr said, chuckling. "Then I'll take a long vacation."

"You might try the desert country down around Tucson in Arizona Territory," Skofer suggested. "It'll be warm and dry there."

"I'd recommend that." Dr. Cadwell nodded.

"I thought I'd like New Orleans or San Francisco, where I could just have fun. I've never had time before." Barr smiled.

"Don't rush off too soon," Root said. "There'll be a conference tomorrow after the ceremony, and no doubt a new candidate will be picked."

"Who do you like?" Barr smiled.

"I'd say it's a toss-up between old George Crook and young George Armstrong Custer. Whoever makes the biggest show in clearing out the Sioux will be our next president."

The lieutenant arrived, nodded to the cook, and took his place at the head of the table.

"Talking politics?" he asked.

"Just pickin' our next president," I said.

"Why not go direct and crown Cornelius Vanderbilt? He's the boss," the lieutenant said.

"True," Barr replied, "but we must run through the rigamarole every four years."

"Are you saying a poor man of humble origins cannot be elected to the presidency?" Root glared at the lieutenant, who speared a fried steak from a platter and passed it on.

"No. The poorer and humbler the better," young Falls said with a smile, "but just let him try to raise up the poor and humble, and you'll see the eastern bankers bury him in bad press stories. All of a sudden he's not poor, he's a thief. Or he's not humble anymore, he's stupid. Right, Mr. Barr?"

"That's a fair assessment." Barr nodded, coughing politely into a clean bandanna.

"Now don't get excited," Cadwell said nervously.

"I disagree," Root snapped, "and the general's tragic death should not be subjected to casual frivolity."

"Seems like Snow's murder is connected up with the general's," I said quietly.

"It's best for all concerned to forget the whole thing," the lieutenant said. "I just want to see the ceremony done according to the book and then close the curtains."

"I agree with the lieutenant," Sarah said, looking over at him. "Whoever's guilty needn't be hounded forever."

"I wouldn't be quite that strong about it," Cadwell said, "but I'd hate to see anyone suffer for such an act of . . . generosity."

"I'll stay with the majority." Barr grinned.

"Don't be too hasty," Root growled, his chubby, bulldoggy features out of kilter. "We must respect the law at all times."

"That's the silliest thing I've ever heard," Dr.

Cadwell said irritably. "I say let sleeping dogs lie, and—"

"Bury the hatchet?" I couldn't resist it.

The doctor glared at me and said strongly, "Look, Mr. Benbow, we've all been subject to a great strain. We're all tired and nervous, and hardly rational—"

"All right," the lieutenant interrupted, "most of us agree, and the majority rules. No more talk."

"Before we lock the barn door," I said mildly, "does anyone know where Snow's buckskin blouse went?"

I was trying to watch all their faces, but it wasn't easy. The lieutenant looked bitter. Barr's face was too pale to read. Cadwell's handsome features sagged visibly, and he looked at his plate. Root's lopsided jaw trembled so that his plump cheeks shook. Sarah's heart-shaped face flushed, and she frowned.

"Why?" Root demanded.

"There's a reason that shirt is missin'," I said.

"I suggest since you haven't got anything better to do, you go look for it," the lieutenant said stonily, rising from the table, putting an end to my questions.

"Mighty fine belly-packin' material," Skofer said, spearing another steak with his fork, and everyone stared at him as if he'd just arrived from under a rock.

There was something I didn't like about the way Lieutenant Falls was draggin' a wet blanket across my trail, and I followed him down toward the monument where the burial detail waited for orders.

The lieutenant looked down at the open graves, each with a neat gunny sack containing a reasonable number of unidentified bones.

"How many, Sergeant?" the lieutenant asked.

"The general and six from here, and there's eighteen from the lower village, sir."

"Very well, Sergeant." The lieutenant made up his mind. "Fill in the graves and set out twenty-five markers on a grid."

"Sir," the sergeant said stiffly, "six markers by four leaves one left over. Where should I put the extra marker?"

The lieutenant flushed angrily, paused to think, and said sternly, "Put the general's marker front and center, where it should be."

"Front and center. Yes, sir."

"It seems that no matter how hard I try to do something properly, it always goes wrong." Falls grinned and shook his head. "How can I make a living outside?"

"You won't be short of money," I said. "What difference does it make?"

"But surely I'm worth something to someone . . ." He frowned worriedly.

"You talkin' about marriage, family, workin' on a project?"

"I suppose so," he said, like he wanted me to tell him what to do.

"I have a couple dreams," I said quietly. "One is to go to a little valley in California and raise horses. That's a dream I know somethin' about."

"The other?"

"The same valley, only plant grape vines and build a winery."

"I don't know anything about either." The lieutenant sighed with disappointment.

"You can learn," I said. "You're still young. Hire an expert and get started."

"But I don't want to do it alone."

"Find a good strong woman who's a good learner, too. Try a schoolmarm. They're good, and they never quit on you."

"Thanks, Benbow, I'll think about it," he murmured, his eyes lost in thought.

I figured that even if he was ten years behind himself, he was still young enough to grow up.

"Won't be easy," I said.

"I've never found anything easy yet," he said. "Do you think I killed the general?"

He slipped it in so neatly. I looked at his baby-faced features with the sloping chin and wondered if I'd overlooked something.

"You're still on the list. Why?"

"I've noticed how you can talk so easily about a lot of things like cattle and winemaking, but whenever there's talk of murder, you're listening."

"That's my job."

"How many men have you killed, Mr. Benbow, aside from the war?"

The question made me think of Fogarty, and I said, "Too many. I don't keep count."

"Then why isn't your name at the top of your list?" he asked, watching me closely.

"Because I know damned well I didn't do it."

146

"Or your friend, Skofer, or both of you? Why not? He roasted you as much as the rest of us."

"I don't kill anyone sleepin'," I said flatly. "Neither would Skofer. No, the kind of man that I'm lookin' for has a big hate inside him, but he's nervous. He was afraid he'd botch it, and that's why he kept choppin'. He was afraid he wasn't doin' it right."

"Someone like me, then," the lieutenant said, his face paling.

"Like you, Root, Barr, or the doctor. Maybe even Sarah Duffy. Underneath they're really not equipped to do the job."

"You left out Minelli," the lieutenant said.

"I'm not sure about Minelli. He's so damned strong, and he knows tools. I can't see him doin' all the extra axe work. One swing would be enough for him."

"But not if he was in a frenzied fury."

"I need that buckskin blouse," I said levelly.

"Why?"

"Because tomorrow's the big day."

"I'm sorry, I don't even know where to look."

"It's somewhere in camp or close by," I said, turning away and walking across to the monument where Minelli stood on his scaffold, layering in another rock.

"Mr. Minelli," I called, "how does the work go?"

"I'm late. Always some son of a bitch wants to shame me," he grumbled.

"You have an uncle in Italy that makes wine?"

"Me?" he asked, as if he didn't understand the question.

"You."

"Hell, yes," he fired back, once he got it through his head I was serious. "My uncle Vito make the best Chianti in all Tuscany."

"Tell the lieutenant about him," I said.

"I ain't got time. I gotta get the damned flagpole up!"

I went back up the slope toward camp, wondering where Skofer had disappeared to.

Sarah still sat at the big table with Barr across from her, but now he had his sketchbook out and was working away with pen and ink. She held still for him but let her eyes turn toward me.

"She's a wonderful model," Barr said, pleased. "Maybe I should give up being a hired flack and try being a serious artist."

"You've certainly got the talent for it," I said, looking over his shoulder at the likeness, which was accurate enough—but even more, it reflected the deep-seated integrity I saw every time I looked at her.

"I used to have ambitions that way," he muttered, not pausing with his pen strokes, "but somehow those early dreams got shuffled aside."

"Seen Skofer?"

"He told the doctor he wasn't feeling well," Barr said.

"Thanks," I said, and I went on around toward the daugherty.

"Now let me speak a few words about our fallen

148

leader, General Frederick Falls, who, though born in poor and humble circumstances, rose up through the ranks because of his ability to be cool under fire, courageous when charging forward against the perfidious Santa Anna in the war for the liberation of the great southwest territory . . ."

Lifted and mingled on the wind, August Root's oratory drifted by, but along with it I heard the unmistakable braying of my tone-deaf partner.

"Sometimes I drink whiskey, sometimes I
      drink rum,
Sometimes I drink brandy, at other times
      none . . ."

His voice warbled high and low like he was trying to drive the coyotes out of the country.

"But if I get boozy, my whiskey's my own,
And them that don't like me can leave me
      alone . . ."

I reckoned he'd finally located a source of fuel for his bravura tenor.

The side door was open, and I heard Skofer burble, "Here's to your good health, Doc," and after a pause, "What else would you like to hear?"

"Mr. Skofer," I heard the doctor's complaining voice, "please give me back that bottle. You said—"

"I know a real purty one, Doc, that'll make you think of gliding waters and singing nightingales . . ."

"Mr. Skofer, please—"

Ignoring the pleas of the doctor, Skofer launched into another song, only this one was a different kind of ballad.

"I'm goin' back to Texas, where the whiskey is red,
And drink a few jugs 'til I'm out of my head . . ."

There was a pause for a quick gurgle, and before the doctor could start complaining Skofer finished up in a high, keening falsetto.

"And when I return, it will be in the fall
To see the bright leaves and hear the geese call . . ."

I thought I'd poke my head in and ask if there was any left in the jug, but I was pretty sure Skofe would say no, selfish liar that he is.

I drifted over the slope toward Sarah's tent, thinking she might be finished posing for her portrait and have some idea where to locate the buckskin blouse.

She wasn't there, but Sergeant Price and a middle-sized corporal with a black frizzly beard were.

Before I could ask what business they had in her camp, the sergeant rasped out, "I figured you'd show up here. Seen the look in your eye."

"There never was a look in my eye."

"You're here, though," the beefy sergeant said, his broad, battered, drink-raddled face grinning wisely.

"I'm here," I nodded. "What do you want?"

"We've got a mighty attractive proposition for you, Mr. Benbow." The sergeant smiled expansively and winked at the corporal.

"I'm listening," I said, puzzled by the heavy-shouldered, big-bellied trooper who, from the look of him, had cost the taxpayers about a thousand times what he was worth in pilferage alone.

"It's the reward," the sergeant said, eyeing me closely. "We want to split it with you."

"You know who murdered the general?"

"Sure we do, but we got to dress it up a little." The sergeant grinned. "We got him, but he just don't know it yet."

"Doesn't know what?"

"That he killed the general!" The corporal stole the joke out from under the beefy sergeant, and the sergeant glared at him.

"I don't need another victim," I said.

"It ain't like he's a victim. He's just a private that's a little short of furniture in the upstairs parlor, you know what I mean," the sergeant said, sticking his face close to mine so I could see his jagged front teeth.

"Some recruiter back east sold him to the army, and the army's been tryin' to get rid of him ever since," the corporal said in his quiet feather-duster voice.

"Has he confessed to anything yet?" I asked, holding onto the tail of the big red kite starting to fly in my head.

"When we make the deal he'll confess to anything you want," the sergeant said.

"I can't make that kind of a deal."

"Why not? We kill two birds with one stone. You have the killer, we get rid of the dummy."

"No, thanks," I said, not tired, but a little sick.

"What the hell's the matter with you, old-timer?" The sergeant looked at me like I'd insulted him.

"I'll give you half the reward if you'll turn up Snow's buckskin blouse," I said, "but I won't give a plugged nickel for your private."

"Look, Benbow"—the corporal grinned—"it ain't like he'll feel anything if they hang him. He'll just be happy as a blind dog knockin' around in a meat house if we tell him it's for his friends. He just loves to please."

"I want no part of it."

"You still mad at me for punchin' you down the other night?" the sergeant growled, his eyes turning mean.

"You were just doin' what the general told you, sort of like what your private would do if you told him."

"I ain't no damn dummy like him!" The sergeant's voice went a little lower and slower.

He wasn't armed. I couldn't very well shoot him, and I wanted to save my fight for somethin' worthwhile.

"I'm not callin' you names," I said quietly. "Best we just forget the whole thing."

"I'm thinkin' you might tell the lieutenant," the corporal said. He was at least shrewder than the sergeant.

"Why bother?"

"You would, though, wouldn't you? I seen big-mouthed recruits like you come in, and after I pounded 'em into mush they shaped up into my kind of soldier," the sergeant said.

"You're not shapin' me up, mister," I said, trying to back off.

They were a pair, though, that had learned to move together, two on one, and while one side of my head was saying draw and shoot the sonsabitches as quick as possible, the other was saying you're all done with killing people. As I did a hop to the left to avoid the corporal's tripping boot, the sergeant's right hand caught me on the jaw. If he hadn't taken his time rearing back and winding it up, it would have taken my head off. As it was, I was moving aside as it landed, and half its force was cushioned away. Half was not near enough. When he reared back and got set for another big boomer I grabbed the corporal and whirled him in between us, then stumbled backwards, clear of the big right hand.

The corporal kept on turning and made a dive for my legs.

They'd worked it other times, I realized. The corporal knocks a man's legs out from underneath him, and the sergeant follows with a boot to the head or the belly, it wouldn't make much difference.

The corporal caught my heel, but by then I knew what to expect and did a backward roll, coming to my feet facing the charging sergeant.

I put my head down and slammed forward, the crown of my head catching him on the point of his jaw. I heard his teeth rattle and grind together like marbles in a poke.

He grunted and backed up. I threw a low left hook to his liver and brought around my right which connected with his already ruined ear.

I threw the hook again and shortened the right, but he didn't go down.

Suddenly my legs went out from under me as the corporal came diving at my knees from behind.

I gave him an elbow in the face that splayed out his nose and made him scream, but it was no help when the sergeant bulled forward with his practiced heavy-soled boot.

I tried to move my head away from the blow and grab his ankle, but there was too much of it, and my hands lost power when the boot crashed against my cheekbone.

Falling down into the depths of oblivion, I heard through distant thunderclouds, "I will shoot to kill!"

It was the voice of someone I knew, I thought, a nice lady who used to be a farm girl before she became a teacher. I just couldn't quite remember her name.

"Leave him be and git!"

I thought, Sam, old-timer, now is the time to hang on and come back swinging, but there was nothing to hang onto, and I felt too tired to lift my little finger.

"They're gone, Sam," she said. "Let's get you in the shade."

She guided me as I crawled slowly over to her tent, but the dark, swirling fog filled up my head when I was

154

halfway in, and I went down. She kept on talking and coaxing and pulling until I was stretched out on her bedroll. Then she tugged off my boots, undid my gun belt, loosened the top button on my jeans, and said, "Lie quiet."

In a moment I felt a soft, wet cloth touch my face, and the fresh coolness of it pushed the fog away a little so that I knew pretty much where I was and how I got there. Now the thing to do was get back to my own camp and listen to Skofer yodel while I healed.

"That's a very nasty scrape, Sam," she said. "His boot, I suppose."

I didn't much care about a little scrape. I was just glad he wasn't a raftsman with steel caulks screwed into his boot soles.

She went out for a minute or two, and I faded away.

Something stirred beside me as I drifted up out of a gray unremembered dream, and I felt the soft, long hair against my stubbly chin.

—Oh, God! I thought, maybe I'm in a bear's den, and I waited a while until I felt her breathing against my sore breastbone.

Knowing it wasn't a bear, I bravely drifted off again.

The next time I had a lucid thought it was a feverish dream that my left hand was touching bare skin.

This time I didn't think it was anything but plump and fine. Her hair lay on my chest, and I had the feeling that the bare skin touching my hand was not the only bare skin in the tent.

There is a point that nature has figured out where a

man loses all the sense he's packed into his head for many years and becomes a totally different kind of animal bent on reproduction.

I figure the man hasn't got too much to say about it, that the female senses her own need and right then some sort of invisible reata loops out and figure-eights the poor cowboy by the head and front feet before he can get set to run.

You can think all you want beforehand and reason for days afterward, but once she throws the loop your thinker moves downstairs.

She rolled on her side, and I felt her mouth burning on my throat. Slowly turning on her back, her soft, silently pulsing lips touched mine. I was enjoying a really nice dream, just a long, slow, back-and-forth rocking chair by the fireside kind of dream, but when she squeaked in my ear it changed into something else.

Sometime later she whispered, "Sam . . ."

"Yes'm?"

"Thank you."

"No'm, it's the other way around," I murmured.

"I was damned if I was going to die a virgin," she whispered with a little giggle, and then she breathed out a happy "Wheeee!"

— 11 —

THE HEROES OF STILL A MIGHTIER STRUGGLE, THE MAR-
tyrs of an immortal defense of national honor, are
falling fast 'til all are gone, victims of a thankless
war . . ."

Dreaming of a political windbag instead of the
perfectly plump Sarah Duffy, fortunately I woke up
and discovered it wasn't Mr. Horsefeathers, it was the
unintelligible groaning, whimpering Skofer Haavik.

His hands and arms were twined like wild grape
vines around his head, and except for plaintive cries
he looked long dead of alcohol poisoning.

"Swallow some wolf bait, Skofe?" I asked softly.
"Want me to get the doc?"

"Please . . . be . . . quiet," he whispered through
dry, caked lips.

"Best thing for wolf bait poison is to swaller down

157

all the rotten green pork fat you can," I said. "Just hold your nose and poke it down—"

"Yipe!" He threw off his blanket and hopped off downwind to puke.

Crawling back on hands and knees, his face a swampy white mask of pain, he whimpered, "Damn, damn, damn, never again . . . poor Skofe . . . never ever again . . ." He crawled under the blanket, and a greasy sweat broke out on his lined forehead as he closed his fearful eyes.

"You look like you're ready for burial," I said. "I'll ask the lieutenant if he's got room for a latecomer."

"You know what he'll say, though . . ." Skofer croaked.

"He'll say your corpse is so full of poison it ought to be put on exhibition as a warning to the youth of America."

"You . . . you . . . Brutus . . ."

Once I knew he could talk back I set my mind on something Sarah had said the evening before. It had to do with the missing blouse. She'd been rambling in fits and spurts of vague ideas, then she'd said, "The blouse is gone because Snow's killer wasn't able to drag him all the way down to the river . . ."

Made sense. That incriminating blouse was a lot easier to hide than the body. I had no more than six hours to find it.

As I ambled over the raked-clean battlefield in the dew-drenched dawn I figured if the killer was in that much of a hurry, he wouldn't have time to get clear over the river.

If he was in a hurry, the blouse would have to be someplace close by, say between where the body was found and the far side of the slope where the daugherty was parked.

But that included a lot of wagons, soldiers, and civilian camps and didn't help out much. In fact, it made me dizzy, and I figured I shouldn't try to be galloping my brain without feeding it first.

By the time I reached the camp the coffee was made and the bacon frying.

Lieutenant Falls was up earlier even than me. His good morning was brief, and he eyed the scrape on my cheekbone without comment.

The sergeant stood at ease nearby, and the lieutenant gave him his orders. "Take a man with you and go up the trail until you meet General Sheridan's entourage. Then act as his personal escort in returning here. That should be close to noon."

"Yessir." The sergeant saluted. I noticed a couple discolored knobs on his heavy face and felt better.

Gerald Barr and the doctor came into camp together, the doctor looking like he'd stayed up all night trying to get his medicinal brandy away from Skofer, but Barr looked better. Freshly shaved, his pale yellow hair brushed to a shine, the color in his cheeks had spread out and diluted so that he looked almost like a healthy outdoorsman.

"You're lookin' much improved, Mr. Barr," I said as he accepted a cup of coffee from the black cook.

"Feel better, too. The good doctor finally hit on just the medicine I need."

159

"What do you call it?"

"It's a blend of the tinctures of laudanum and iron with an addition of sweet nitre," Barr said. "I slept well last night, the first time since we arrived here."

"You let yourself get run down working day and night," Dr. Cadwell scolded. "You had me worried for a while."

"That life of trying to meet the general's every whim is over," Barr said. "I've decided to set up a studio in New York where I can paint portraits or western scenes and probably make a decent living."

"Looks like a rosy future for you," I said. "It's a good thing the general died, or you'd have been wore down to the nubbin of a corn cob."

"That seems a month ago, doesn't it?" Barr nodded thoughtfully. "He was a hard man at times, but always generous. I'll miss him."

"Yes, they don't make men like him very often." The doctor nodded reverently.

"Maybe we're talkin' about two different animals," I said, puzzled. "I remember him as one hundred percent pure quill son of a bitch."

"Sometimes he had to be a disciplinarian. Otherwise he would never have achieved such greatness," Dr. Cadwell said.

"Are you making any progress toward bringing in his killer?" Barr asked. "It won't do to leave the crime unpunished."

"I think I'll have it tacked together soon as I find Snow's blouse."

"Can you do it before the ceremony?" the doctor asked, his eyes looking off somewhere.

"Did I hear you right?" August Root stepped in between the doctor and the cook and held out his hand for a cup of coffee. "You're going to give us the killer?"

"Was it Sickle?" the lieutenant asked, coming forward.

"No, it wasn't Sickle or Snow. I'll let you know in a few hours," I lied, figuring to stir things up some since I was getting nowhere by just looking around.

"Could it be a person of female persuasion?" Sarah smiled at me, her face soft and radiant, her eyes dancing with secret laughter.

"I'd best not talk too much about it until I have all the evidence."

"Suppose you don't find the evidence?" the lieutenant asked, his eyes fixed on mine.

"I can name the person, but I doubt if you'd give me the reward for that," I said.

"Yes, I need more than just a hunch." He nodded slowly. "We need conclusive evidence."

"It would give me great pleasure," Root said expansively, "if we could have an execution by firing squad before all the dignitaries."

"Speaking of dignitaries," the lieutenant said hurriedly, "I've got to get Minelli moving faster."

"The place looks rather nice now, doesn't it?" Barr said, sweeping his hand to indicate the battlefield in the big bend of the river.

161

"You ought to paint a picture of it," I said.

"As soon as the monument is finished." Barr smiled at me.

"At least the flagpole is up," Dr. Cadwell said, settling down to his breakfast of flapjacks and bacon.

"And Old Glory will soon fly over this sacred and hallowed ground," Root said portentously. "Doesn't that make your heart thrill, Sarah?"

"I'm afraid not, Mr. Root. A black flag with a skull and crossbones on it would be more honest."

"My dear lady,"—Root flushed—"that's blasphemous, traitorous talk. For your own good you should be more careful what you say."

"You make a very good living blathering about that flag," she said with a chuckle. "That's all you're worried about."

"Now let's not quarrel," the doctor said quietly, breaking up the exchange.

"Just let me say, please, that after Mr. Root's speech I think somebody ought to get up and tell the truth about how my brother was left to die by a cowardly, politically ambitious officer."

"You wouldn't dare!" Root stood on his toes, trying and failing to tower over her.

"I just might!" she snapped back.

"I warn you clearly, Miss Duffy," Root grated. "You are unbalanced, and you will end up in a hospital for the insane if you don't keep your mouth shut!"

"Mr. Root," I said quietly, with my right hand balled up, "maybe you better be the one who shuts up."

162

He saw my face and my fist and took a step backward, his right hand moving inside his coat without thinking. When he was well clear he sneered, "You're a big bulldogger out here, but I wish you'd come to Washington. I'd like to show you a few tricks."

"Somehow I have the feeling a slimy thief like you won't make it back to Washington," I said.

I enjoyed seeing his pointy jaw drop in surprise. Somehow he had the idea that he was indispensable to the nation and untouchable by its citizens, and when he saw himself as a mortal swindler he couldn't believe it.

Walking off down the hill to our camp, I found Skofer on the road to recovery. The swampy green was gone from his pallid features, and his bloodshot eyes were open.

"Don't say anything." He held up a trembling hand.

"Not me. I wouldn't waste my time preachin' a sermon to a habitual sinner like you."

He hung his head, waiting to get it over with.

"I'm just sayin' I can go it alone. I don't need any help in windin' up the whole shebang in the next four hours. All I've got to do is find Snow's blouse or confess I'm as big a windbag as August Root."

"I'll think on it," Skofer groaned, his eyes still closed. I waited without speaking, and he peered up at me with one eye like a shamed old hound dog and murmured, "It hurts to think."

"You think, or I'll keep on talkin'."

"It has to be close," he said tentatively. "Whoever

killed Snow should have thrown him into the river and he'd be gone. But he didn't, so he was in a hurry, or Snow had hurt him so he couldn't do it. That enough?"

"I already got that figured," I said, thinking that between Sarah and him I wouldn't have to do anything except listen.

"We've got to walk the perimeter," he said weakly, "cover the whole area. Give me half an hour."

"I'll get started, you take your time."

"Thanks, Sam," he said piteously, clutching at his scrawny gray head.

From our camp I walked an arc around the rise that overlooked the battlefield.

Bushy-bearded Corporal Hansen, who'd sided with the sergeant the day before, stood at ease in front of the lead tent of Company B. The other tents were set up in orderly rows, but most of the troopers were off currying and brushing their all-gray horses in a rope corral near the river.

"What's your business here, mister?" he said, lifting his carbine to port.

"Lookin' around."

"You ain't in Company B, you don't get to look around," he said.

"Did you know Snow?" I asked.

"I seen him, but not to talk to," he said. "Move along. You belong in officer country."

"Was Snow ever over here talkin' to somebody or tradin' goods or somethin'?"

"Not to my knowledge," he said, trying to sound like the stiff-upper-lip military.

"What's goin' on, Lafe?" asked a big young kid who looked like he'd be better off behind a plow. His upper lip hung down over the lower one.

"See this jasper, Clete? He was sayin' yesterday you killed the general."

"Ah, you know I wouldn't do that." The big kid with the strange eyes smiled slowly.

"That's what we told him, but he said he was goin' to hang you for it."

"You're funnin' me again, ain't you, Lafe?" Clete said, nodding.

"Did you ever talk to that halfbreed Snow?" I asked.

"Some. I think he wanted to sell somethin', but I don't remember . . ." Clete said slowly, staring off into space, his upper lip drooping low again.

"You see?" The corporal grinned at me. "Our offer still stands."

"Reckon not." I shook my head. "But don't shoot me just because I'm slow to say yes."

"Hell, we wouldn't shoot you, would we, Clete?" the corporal laughed. "Not unless you started sayin' the wrong things to the lieutenant."

"That's right," Clete said, nodding and nodding.

"I'll let you know tomorrow," I said, and I moved off before they remembered tomorrow we wouldn't be here.

Minelli's wagon stood outside the regular perimeter, but I moseyed over anyways. Of them all, Minelli had the most compelling reason to kill the general, and I couldn't scratch his name off the list. I felt fairly certain that if Minelli had not killed the general, it was because someone else had beaten him to it.

Minelli's blankets were rolled up underneath the wagon bed. A small iron frying pan that had never been washed sat on a rock by the ashes of his small fire. I looked through a flap in the wagon canvas and hauled out a gunny sack that turned out to be full of dirty, ragged overalls and shirts. I put it all back and unrolled the blankets. No buckskin blouse there.

Coming around the rise, still not far from the tents of Company B, stood the empty spare ambulance where Snow had been locked up for a while. The door was still barred from the outside.

I lifted the bar and looked at the bare benches and empty floor.

Closing the door, I went farther on around to the tent where I'd spent part of the evening before.

Surely Sarah wouldn't have hidden the blouse, I thought, but then maybe someone else had put it where no one would look. Got to do it.

She stood in the doorway, surprised by my appearance, watching me with puzzlement.

"You're early, Sam," she said, smiling.

"Ma'am," I said, touching my hat, "you told me to look through the whole camp, and that's what I'm doin'."

"You mean you want to search my tent and buckboard?" She frowned. "Don't you trust anyone?"

166

I could see there was nothing in the buckboard except her team's harness, and I said, "Suppose somebody figured your place would be perfect?"

She looked at me distantly and shook her head. "I don't believe it, but go ahead and look."

She stepped aside, and I looked at the familiar bed quilts all made up neatly and poked at a large carpetbag that held her spare clothes. I put my hand on the cherrywood hope chest that I knew held her brother's bones.

"I won't unlock that chest," she said firmly. "No one could have opened it."

"Yes'm," I said, stepping back out. "I'm sorry if I've overstepped."

"You're a strange, quiet man, Mr. Benbow," she said, backing away. "You're also merciless, aren't you?"

"No, ma'am," I said, figuring the best thing to do when confronted with a female that thinks she's got you hogtied and ready to cut and brand is to go away quietly, but go.

"You can be replaced, Mr. Benbow," she said softly to my back.

"Yes'm." I touched my hat again and moved on.

The doctor and Gerald Barr were sitting at a camp table under a tarp stretched out from the side of their daugherty.

From the distance I could hear scattered phrases of Root's speech pinned on the wind.

"Morning, gents," I said, and Barr looked up from his sketch pad. I noticed the doctor holding his pose, and I quickly added, "Go on ahead, I'm just lookin' around for that buckskin blouse."

"You want to search the daugherty?" Barr asked, going back to concentrating on his portrait. "You're welcome."

"Thanks." I nodded and went inside the big converted ambulance, riffled through the bunks, checked the cabinets and suitcases and bags. After forcing the locks I found a couple of interesting documents in Root's satchel. Barr's pigskin valise contained a bank book with some big numbers in it. There was a curling iron in the doctor's kit that I thought passing strange until I recalled how beautifully his long hair and sideburns waved down to his collar.

Putting Root's documents inside my jumper, I went on out and said, "Won't be long before the circus starts."

"Yes, we'll have to change clothes," Barr murmured, not looking up from the work. "Find anything?"

"Nope."

I looked at the view from the daugherty that took in about half the battlefield and the riverbend and saw Minelli pushing his wheelbarrow at a run.

"Joe Minelli's cuttin' it pretty fine with his monument," I said.

"Yes." Barr nodded. "The lieutenant tried to lend him a couple of men, but he absolutely refused."

"He's proud and hotheaded. Can't argue with a man like that," I said, and I added, "Sorry to bother you."

As I turned and moved on around the arc toward the river Barr said, "Anytime."

"Here you are, you beggarly, treacherous rascals, for years you have lived on our bounty and eaten of our bread. You are well fed, well cared for; you, your papooses and ponies are fat and independent; but you miss the grand revel in blood, scalps, and trophies. You have no grievance, but the love of raping and warfare is the ruling passion, and you must take a hand against the Great White Father, whom your treaty binds you to obey and honor . . .

Root was going strong, telling Wide Bear and his people just what he thought of them a year after they were all dead.

The crying wind lifted his oratory and carried it south. I sort of wished the wind would change and blow it all northerly where Crazy Horse and Sitting Bull could hear it.

There were no more wagons or ambulances to search, and I'd found nothing more interesting than a curling iron.

Skofer stood over by the monument watching Minelli mix mortar in his wheelbarrow.

Recovering, his face kept working around in strange, nervous grimaces, and he kept his hands tucked into his back pockets.

"Find anything?"

"Nope."

The lieutenant rode up on his gray horse and asked Minelli, "How are you coming along?"

"I'm doing good if people will just let me do my

job," Minelli growled. "Everybody got to pick on the dago."

The lieutenant was in full dress uniform with gold epaulets and braid on his sleeves, his saber on the left side hooked to his belt, his carbine in its scabbard under his right leg.

The gray gelding shone like polished pewter from a morning of grooming. Its mane and tail were combed into waterfalls, the tack soaped and buffed to a shine.

"Goin' to do a drill for the bigwigs?" I asked.

"It's part of the general's plan." He nodded. "The general's aide-de-camp will carry his guidon and lead the general's horse with the boots backwards in the stirrups. We'll come in fours from upriver, do a fours right, and halt just behind the grave markers. We'll present arms, then go to at ease while the heavyweights void themselves of their speeches. The bugler will play 'The General,' we'll come to attention, present arms, and fire six volleys at the sky. The bugler will play taps, then everyone can go home."

"Got it worked out nicely, but you forgot the wreaths. You can't have a ceremony without a wreath."

"The wreaths will be presented by Senator McReynolds and General Sheridan. I asked Miss Sarah Duffy if she'd care to place a wreath on the monument, but she refused."

"She's a determined lady," I replied.

"But rather attractive," he said, his voice changing. "Don't you think?"

"I'd say so," I said agreeably. "I hear she used to teach school, too."

"That's definitely an asset." He smiled broadly and rode up the slope toward camp.

Looking at the monument, I saw that Minelli had started his stone pyramid on top of the square-shaped shaft. He could probably finish it in an hour with plenty of time left over.

"You have the plaque?" I asked Minelli, who was loading up his hod with mortar.

"That plaque tells lies," he said shortly. "We don't need it."

"The lieutenant agree?"

"He said throw it inside the monument," Minelli growled.

He glared at me for a second, then lifted the hod to his shoulder and climbed up on his scaffold.

"What are you talking about?" Skofer asked weakly.

"It don't matter," Minelli said from the scaffold, setting the hod on a rickety waist-high platform. "You think I build a real monument for the man that killed my brother's son?"

"Would somebody please invite me to the discussion?" Skofer sighed in frustration.

"Joe figures a flood will come up next spring and take away the monument and grave markers so it'll all be like it used to be, except, of course, for the Indians," I explained.

"So what is he doing wrong?" Skofer looked at the stone shaft. "It looks plenty strong to me."

"You should have looked at it earlier. It's really just a shell of stone that's been filled in with dirt, and he's dumped the plaque in there, too."

"No one will ever know as soon as I put on the *capa,*" Minelli said stolidly, slathering mortar on a rock edge.

"Just a shell for show," Skofer said tightly, looking into my eyes and nodding. "A real shell game."

"What did you say yesterday, Joe, about people tryin' to shame you?" I asked quietly.

"That's what I said," Minelli growled, setting the first rock of his pyramid.

"How do they do that, Joe?" I asked, looking at Skofer, who was smiling like the cat with a yellow tail feather in its mouth.

"They pull down some rocks after I'm gone. You do that?" He glared at me. "You fellas think that's a good joke to play on the dumb dago?"

"No, Joe, I don't know who did it, but I bet I know why," I said.

Skofer grinned and climbed up on the scaffolding.

"How did you guess?" I asked, following after him.

"Logic and simple deduction. It had to be here, but I thought the monument was solid rock," Skofer said, and to a surprised Minelli he murmured, "Excuse me, Mr. Minelli, I've got to look in here."

"Stay back!" Minelli roared.

Before he could take a swing at Skofer a heavy-caliber bullet came screaming in between the two of them.

Minelli waited a second, puzzled, then with wide-open bulging eyes dived off the scaffold and flattened himself behind the monument. Skofer, quick as a barked squirrel, landed on top of him, and I did a corkscrew dive off to the left and squirmed alongside.

"How the hell can I work like this?" Minelli said bitterly. "They ask too much from an artist!"

"How much longer will it take?" I asked, to fill in the time before I had to stick my head around the corner.

"Half an hour . . . just four rocks. I already got 'em cut."

"Okay, Joe, let's do it this way . . . if I can get up there to the camp alive, you help Skofer dig that buckskin blouse out of your monument, and then he'll help you finish the top, okay?"

"I ain't movin' till you're up there," Joe said.

═══ **12** ═══

THE BLACK COOK POKED HIS ROUND FACE SLOWLY around the side of a water barrel, saw the six-gun in my hand, and ducked back.

I was sweating not only from the charge up the slope, but from crossing so much open ground with a sharpshooter somewhere up there, and I was mad at myself for being short of breath.

"What the hell's goin' on, Cookie?" I holstered the Colt and scanned the whole outlook from our camp clear around to the daugherty.

"Don't ask me, boss," the cook said, poking his head out again, his eyes round as white china saucers.

"Do you know where that shot came from?"

"No, sir," he said, slowly standing up. "I just heard somethin' makin' a straight coattail right by my ear like the after-clap from the devil."

174

"Anyone else here?"

"No, sir. Everybody done et and gone."

I looked over the scene again and waved my hat to signal Skofer and Minelli.

Taking that shot was such a muddle-headed thing to do, it had to be from panic. Who was that nervous? I watched the whole hillside as Joe climbed up on his scaffold and rooted in the dirt he'd piled inside the monument. I waited until he pulled out the cream-colored leather garment.

While Skofer carried it up the slope toward me Minelli went back to work. In a few minutes he'd cement the pyramid-shaped cap in place. Give him time to tear down his scaffolding, and he'd be on his way back to Italy.

One thing the sharpshooter had done was to take Joe Minelli off my list.

That list was now fined down to Lieutenant Falls, Gerald Barr, Doc Cadwell, August Root, and maybe Sarah Duffy.

One of the five, maybe two of the five—hell, maybe they'd all taken a whack at the general and ganged up on Snow.

But one of them had cracked when he saw us looking inside the monument. Someone panicked and tried to stop the finding of Snow's blouse.

"Who the devil is shooting in camp?" the lieutenant demanded, striding in, his carbine held across his chest at the ready.

"Someone from up this way took a shot at Skofer

while we were poking around the monument," I said, eyeing him thoughtfully. "Where were you?"

"Are you accusing me?"

"No, sir, I just asked where you were."

"I was riding up this way from the aide-de-camp's tent," he said slowly, offering me the saddle gun, "and I haven't fired this for a week."

I took the Spencer and sniffed the barrel. It smelled of oiled steel, nothing else.

"One thing we're not short of is carbines," I said, handing the weapon back.

"Listen, Benbow, don't push too hard," he said tiredly.

Skofer arrived and handed the rumpled blouse to me. "This was inside the monument," he said to the lieutenant.

"You found it!" He smiled, and I almost scratched him off the list just for that.

Spreading open the fringed buckskin garment, I noticed a few grease spots on the front of it that tended to blend into the creamy leather.

"Nothing . . ." I said, turning it over and looking at the back. A couple of dark spots stained the upper left shoulder. I turned it again and dug my fingers into the breast pockets half hidden by the fringe across the chest. A half a plug of tobacco and a bent silver concha in the left one. In the right was a folded square of paper that said Albert Snow was employed as a scout for the Fifth Cavalry and a small buckskin poke containing a brass casing from a .56-50 cartridge, a steel pen nib, a small round mirror, and a hard, fibrous stick or root.

"Mean anything to you, Lieutenant?" I asked, laying the items down on the table.

"Nothing special," he said, sniffing at the casing. "This brass might have a tale to tell, but it looks like all the rest to me."

"Make anything out of it?" I asked Skofer.

"Not exactly. The concha might point to the killer, but there's no one among us wears that sort of thing."

"Damn it, he as much as told me he'd seen the general's killer," I said, aggravated by so many disappointing dead ends. "Then he wouldn't say a word afterward."

"And you think he decided to bleed the person he saw and was killed for it?" the lieutenant asked. "But why all the fuss about this shirt?"

"Good question. The killer had to work fast to get it off the breed, then hide it."

I was disgusted by the whole layout. It seemed every time I turned up something it was small potatoes.

"Maybe it's just the whole blouse. Maybe someone we know made it for him, or bought it for him," Skofer muttered, shaking his head, as baffled as me.

"If you'll excuse me, gentlemen, I've got better things to do than ponder over a dirty tunic," the lieutenant said, a little uppity-biggity, I thought, but I was some raspy myself by then.

After the lieutenant was gone Skofer poked at the small articles with his index finger and shook his head. "It's a bad damn joke."

"The brass casing could point at the lieutenant," I said, "the concha at a woman, the pen nib at the writer, the mirror at the wavy-haired doctor, and if that's not a dried-up dandelion root, I'll eat it."

I picked up the blouse again and turned it inside out. The grease stains on the front had gone all the way through, but the splotches on the back hadn't; otherwise it was unmarked. I looked under the collar for a hidden knife pocket, but I came up empty.

Skofer flipped the concha into the air thoughtfully, caught it, and put it carefully back on the table.

"You think Sarah Duffy's strong enough to strangle that halfbreed with a wire?" he murmured.

"It doesn't take so much strength as it does just being sneaky and quick," I said.

"She could have rolled him into the grave," he muttered thoughtfully.

"But it would be a hell of a job to pull that blouse over his head," I said. "I'd just about say scratch her off, except she is quick, and she is strong."

"The others are all citified folks, except for the lieutenant," Skofe said, "and using that wire is a citified trick."

I slipped the concha into the small poke with the rest of the things, and Skofer said, "Goin' to talk to 'em again?"

"I guess we could pray for a revelation," I grumbled. "There's nothin' else left."

I had the feeling somebody was laughing at me and ready to kill me at the same time.

"You know, Skofe," I said seriously, "it seems like

somebody's straddlin' the fence and can't figure which way to jump."

"The killer?"

"He's a dead serious killer except when he doesn't have time to think."

"He sure wasn't thinking when he took a shot at me," Skofer said, nodding.

"A sewer-rat mind . . ." Skofer nodded agreeably. "I've got the picture of his insides, I just haven't matched it up with the outside yet."

"Indian warfare is, of all warfare, the most danger-ous, the most trying, the most thankless. Not recog-nized by the high authority of the United States Senate as war, it still possesses for the soldier the disadvantages of civilized warfare, with all the horri-ble accompaniments that barbarians can invent and savages execute . . ."

Root's speech was going to be long and tedious, and I hoped I wouldn't have to listen to it again.

As we approached Sarah Duffy's tent the lieutenant and she were so engrossed in their conversation that neither noticed us until Skofer cleared his throat.

We were still too far away to hear what they were saying, but the lieutenant stepped back quickly, like he was a kid caught with his hand in the cookie jar.

I saw that the cherrywood chest, her carpetbag, and her carbine had been packed in the back of the buckboard, and I said, "Leaving so soon?"

"Just getting ready," she said. "The lieutenant has been kind enough to help me."

Jack Curtis

"Will you be goin' back to Indiana?" I asked.

"I haven't decided yet," she said, and, glancing at the lieutenant, she added, "It depends . . ."

"I wish no one would leave until I know who's been killin' people around here," I said.

"I don't see that you can hold anyone," the lieutenant said. "As soon as the ceremony is over this place will be deserted."

"Then who sees that justice is done?"

"The Inspector General will take charge," the lieutenant said. "Starting this afternoon."

"The reward?"

"I shouldn't have spoken so quickly, but it still stands until the ceremony ends."

"Don't you think justice has already been done?" Sarah asked, staring at me.

"Does this mean anything special to you, ma'am?" I asked, bringing out the bent silver concha.

"I've never seen it before," she said. "What is it?"

"It's a Mexican peso that's been hammered into a button."

"No, it means nothing to me." She shook her head.

"Did you happen to see anybody use a carbine this mornin', ma'am?" I persisted, walking over to the buckboard and sniffing the barrel of her Spencer.

"The lieutenant told me that there'd been a rifle discharged accidentally," she said. "You think it was mine?"

"Now, now . . ." I smiled. "Did you see anything unusual?"

She paused to think, started to speak, and changed her mind as quick as an army mule can swap ends.

"No . . . no, I didn't."

"I better say, ma'am, that that halfbreed Snow tried to cover up for the killer and got paid back the hard way."

"I shall be fine," she said stiffly.

"I'll make sure of it." The lieutenant stepped between us.

"Sam"—Skofe spoke quietly, easing me out of my slow-burning anger—"I think we've learned what we wanted here."

"Thank you." I touched my hat and turned away.

"She saw somethin'," I said quietly as we walked on up toward the daugherty.

"Yes, she did," Skofer said, "and she intends to keep silent, and you know why."

Dr. Cadwell sat alone in a camp chair at the small table sorting out pill bottles and packages of bandages, killing time.

Looking up, he smiled. "Greetings on this momentous occasion. Please sit down."

"You're sounding awfully cheerful today," I said.

"It's a day for rejoicing, as far as I am concerned. In a few hours I will tender my resignation to the general's replacement and be on my way."

Glancing at Skofer, he added politely but firmly, "I'm sorry that I have no refreshments to offer you."

I laid the tunic and the contents of the leather poke on the table and asked, "Any of this stuff mean somethin' special to you?"

He studied the small items and said, "Whoever wore that tunic was not strong on hygiene. As for the trinkets, the dandelion root means something."

"How about the pen nib?"

"That, too, could be significant, but Mr. Barr couldn't be involved."

"Someone suggested the mirror might point your way," Skofer said mildly.

Cadwell reddened and nodded. "I suppose some mean-minded person might suggest that."

"Where's Barr?" I asked.

"At your service," Gerald Barr said huskily, coming out of the daugherty.

"Gerald, you should be resting," Doctor Cadwell said, half rising.

"I'm better now," Barr said. Carefully sitting down in a camp chair and looking at me, he asked, "You have some business?"

"Did you hear a shot this mornin'?"

"Yes, somewhere close, but we were both inside. I thought perhaps a soldier was shooting at a buzzard or something."

He noticed the tunic, picked it up, and looked it over. "Could stand a good scrubbing," he said. "Is it important?"

"Maybe," I said. "What about these things?"

"A silver peso, a shell casing, a pen nib, a mirror, and a root . . ." He tried to smile, but his cough caught up with him, and he buried his face in a fresh bandanna until it passed.

"You see, Mr. Benbow," Doc Cadwell said, "why I wish my patient were back in his bunk."

"Bother it," Barr said hoarsely, his eyes watering, "it looks like a fortune teller's collection of charms, doesn't it?" He fingered through the clutter. "A girl, a gunman, possibly a soldier, a writer such as myself, and, as I heard, you relate the mirror to the good doctor. Of course, a root is a Root."

"Says everything and nothing," Skofer said.

"Still have your pen case?" I asked.

"Right where it always is," he said, patting the bulge in his breast pocket.

"As I've said before, Mr. Benbow," Doc Cadwell said, "it really serves no useful purpose for you to continue interrogating people. Real justice has already been done."

"I don't understand any of you people," I said, a little heatedly. "Granted, the general was askin' for it, but there's still a law against murder that's supposed to apply to the rich as well as the poor."

"If you must have a victim," the doctor said carefully, "I would give you August Root, the ranter of the prairie."

"Did you see him fire a carbine this morning?" I asked.

"I'm not saying." The doctor smiled brightly, patting his curls. "I couldn't really identify him because the sun was in my eyes."

"Sam," Skofe said quickly, taking me by the arm and leading me away.

"Okay, Skofe," I said when we were clear, "best you go help Miss Duffy pack up. Make sure nobody's sneakin' up behind her with a wire noose."

"You serious, or are you just trying to get rid of me?" Skofer grumbled.

"There's a scalawag loose," I said softly. "Nobody takes it very seriously because we're all such nice people, but if she saw somethin', she could be next."

"Don't worry about her, then." He nodded his bony little head and started back up the hill.

I turned to listen to the harp of the wind and the rising and falling oratory and moved toward it.

". . . while our savage foes are not only the wards of the nation, supported in idleness, but objects of sympathy with large numbers of people otherwise well informed and discerning . . ."

"Root," I interrupted.

"What?" He turned to face me. "By God, can't I have a little privacy? This speech will be printed in every newspaper in the country. If I could only persuade you to leave me alone, I will be delivered of it without an error in about three hours."

"Sounds like you've got it down to the last flea's belly button," I said. "Mind comin' down to the daugherty? I want to show you somethin'."

"Of all the insufferable impertinence!" he snarled, rearing back on his heels.

"If I arrest you for murder, you won't be givin' any speech today," I said.

"Murder! Good Lord, man—I wouldn't kill my partner!"

"You might, if all his share in the business went to you."

"How do you know that?" he countered hotly.

"I looked through your papers." I smiled at his explosive fury that hadn't an ounce of real anger in it. He was a cold, deliberate plotter, and all the world was his stage to rant and rave upon while deep down he was critically watching the show.

"You broke the lock! You had absolutely no right!" he brayed. "I will have you put under arrest the minute Sheridan arrives!"

"Like I said, I'm goin' to beat you to it if you don't come along like a good little boy."

"What else did you take from my satchel?" he gritted out, his eyes half closed.

"Enough to put you in Fort Leavenworth for about twenty years."

"You can't touch me, Benbow," he snarled. "I warn you!"

"You comin'? Or am I goin' to have to drag you by the ear?"

I took a step toward him, and his hand flirted with his vest button. I wondered if I should shoot him before he made up his mind to go for his derringer.

"Don't try it. You'd be playin' a game I'm good at."

If he made any kind of move, I'd already decided to rush and smother him in a bear hug before he could get the little two-shooter out, break his back, then drop him.

His hand drifted away from his vest.

"You're right," he said. "You play with life and death every day. Why should I take a chance?"

"Remember I gave you a little leeway this time. I won't again," I said as he went by me, heading across the slope toward the daugherty.

"You're an arrogant dandy," he muttered over his shoulder. "You'll overreach yourself one day."

"I just don't understand how you keep these rotten deals so quiet," I said.

"Mr. Benbow"—he stopped and tapped my chest with his index finger—"General Falls was a legend. He was Davy Crockett and George Washington molded into a giant of integrity and patriotism. Who would dare to look into his business affairs?"

"Nobody. So why do you think somebody chopped down his cherry tree?"

"If you ask me," he said intensely, "his son hated him from the day he was born. Not out in the open, mind you, but a deep, treacherous hatred buried deep in his soul, a poison that brought him to patricide."

"At least that notion is different than just scrappin' about who gets the money."

He looked at me hard and long.

"You read my correspondence, too?"

"As long as it was there, I figured you wouldn't mind," I said. "Seems like he was easin' you out—caught you takin' a little extra on the side."

"It was simply a misunderstanding," he said strongly. "We straightened it out as soon as I was aware of his concern."

"How do you manage to move a tract of public land

186

from one department to another department, then into a private corporation?"

"The world has always functioned on greed." He smiled smugly. "The system operates by rewarding the most greedy, either in lower taxes, increased benefits, or social privileges. Everyone running the ship of state gets a little bonus."

"I just bet they do . . ."

We came under the awning stretched out from the daugherty.

The doctor and his patient still sat at the table. The doctor had repacked his bag and placed it on the ground.

Barr didn't look like he'd improved much in my absence, but when he saw us coming he squared back his huddled-over shoulders and tried to look strong as a bull.

The cream-colored leather tunic still lay on the table with the items taken from its pockets.

"I want to show these things to Mr. Root," I said. "Maybe he can see somethin' that makes sense."

"I wish you both luck," Barr said in a low, quiet voice that took no effort.

"What is this?" Root demanded, on his high horse again.

"That's Snow's shirt. These articles were in the pockets, and that's a dandelion root."

"Junk," he said succinctly. "Nothing but junk. Why should I waste precious time on your drollery?"

"Doesn't ring a bell or give you any fresh ideas?" I asked.

"No. None at all."

"The doctor seems to think you took a shot at my partner about an hour ago," I said, watching him closely.

"That, sir, is a goddamn lie!" he yelled so loud I almost believed him.

"I said I wasn't exactly sure," Dr. Cadwell said in a small voice. "You're twisting my words."

"You're determined to destroy me, aren't you?" Root stared at me, his mind running faster than he could speak. "You're a do-gooder, one of those failures who just dream all their miserable lives of dragging down an ambitious man."

"I'm just a stock detective in the wrong place," I said carefully, "but I do like the law to work equal for the rich and the poor."

"They are two different things," Root sputtered. "The rich have rich ways, the poor have poor ways. There's no chance of them being equal."

"When it comes to murder, I think there is," I said.

He seemed to wilt, as if I'd cut off the bubbling energy of his high spirit, and he spread his hands wide. "I can easily pay you the reward you want if you'll just go on about your mundane business, but I'm quite sure your moral character wouldn't accept it."

"Likely that's so."

"I'm curious as to how much it would take to change your mind."

"For sure, you don't have enough," I said.

— 13 —

I LOOKED DOWN THE SLOPE AND SAW THAT MINELLI HAD capped the monument with a pointed top and had set a special iron flagpole behind it. He stepped back to survey his work, and after a moment he shook his head.

"What do you intend to do?" Root broke into my reverie, his eyes hot, his voice trembling.

"Soon as the mucky-mucks arrive I'm goin' to look around for an honest newspaperman."

Root started to laugh, but Barr cut him off.

"It isn't funny. That man Finerty of the Chicago *Times* will be along."

"That's just the man I'm thinkin' about." I smiled. "I'll tell him the facts, give him the file, and say equality and justice for all."

189

I was running a bluff on him, but I hadn't much else. With a few friends and a Philadelphia lawyer he could quash the malfeasance in office charges. He'd have to resign, but Washington was full of defrocked patriots like him still doing their dirty work.

"I'm not going to prison, and I've worked too hard to have to start all over again," Root growled, some of his earlier force returning. "And if you're implying I killed the general, you're badly mistaken. I would never kill the goose with the golden eggs."

"But the goose said that night that he was replacing you. Said you were a real pure quill skunk."

"I would have persuaded him to change his mind the next day, if he'd lived," Root said. "He couldn't have dropped me any more than I could drop him."

"You went out for a walk that night, I remember," Barr said casually.

"What are you saying?" Root exploded again. "I most certainly did not go out for a walk that night."

"Maybe you're right," Barr said vaguely. "Maybe it was another night. The night somebody strangled the halfbreed scout."

"Or both nights . . ." Doc Cadwell said, stroking his long curls absently.

"All of you are trying to lay those murders onto me!" Root blustered. "You'll never bring it off. I'll make you all sweat before this is over!"

"Would you swear in front of a judge that Root went out the night of the general's murder?" I put in.

"It's the simple truth." Barr smiled until his breath caught in his throat and he started coughing.

"How long was he gone?"

"I'd say at least an hour. I couldn't sleep because of this tickle in my throat."

"You are lying!" Root yelled. "All of you, lying!"

"Why didn't you tell me before?" I asked.

"I was on the other side," Barr said. "Now I'm turning over a new leaf and starting with a clean slate."

"You'll play hell proving any of that hogwash," Root snarled. "Now, if you'll excuse me, I've got to change." With deep sarcasm he added, "You don't seem to remember that I've been asked to give the eulogy in front of the most powerful leaders in this land."

He swung up into the daugherty and let the canvas curtains down, and I heard him kick off his boots.

"You and the doctor seem to be agreein' on most everything now," I said to Barr, wondering why.

"We're both resigning from the political arena," the doctor said quietly. "We both would like to regain our self-respect after nearly losing it to General Falls."

I was about to ask them why they were lying, hoping to put them in a panic so they'd blurt out the truth, when I heard the sound of moving cloth. I stared at the canvas-sided wagon, but then I reckoned Root was putting on his fancy suit and silk hat.

"You're not worried that Root's friends might ruin you before you ever get started fresh?" I asked.

"I have no fear of any man now," Barr said huskily.

I noticed the slight swaying of the daugherty as Root moved about and thought, far back in my mind, well, that's normal, and then I thought it's really not so normal, because he had only the space beside his bunk to call his own.

Still intent on conversing with Barr, I noticed in the back of my mind a length of blue steel obscured by the far front wheel of the wagon. Then it dawned on me that it was not a part of the wagon, that it was a standard cavalry .56-50 carbine barrel aimed directly at me.

I didn't even have time to yell. I started to jerk aside as smoke erupted from the wagon wheel, and I felt the instant burn of the heavy bullet across my ribs, spinning me sidewise as I tried to dive for the ground.

The wagon wheel made a perfect rest for the carbine except when the target moved too far to one side. Then the sharpshooter couldn't train the barrel around the heavy hickory spoke and would have to disengage and try for a free shot.

I wasn't waiting for another.

As the rifleman jacked in another shell, pulled the carbine out of the spokes, and swung the barrel to his right, ready to make a close, easy shot, I drew my Colt and fired three times, chopping off splinters from the spokes and black oak hub, hoping my lead would find an open space.

I heard a grunt like that of a bear falling out of a bee tree, and the carbine barrel jacked upwards as it bloomed with smoke and fire and lead again.

I lay on my burning side facing the wagon, elbows on the ground, both hands on the walnut grips of the

Colt, holding it steady on the dark form behind the wagon wheel.

It moved, and I yelled, "No more, Root."

It moved again, and I slowly squeezed the trigger, sending a lump of lead into the center of the kneeling man.

The eight hundred pounds of muzzle velocity snapped him over backwards like a mule had just kicked him in the chest with both hind legs.

I crawled under the wagon tongue to the front wheel and saw Root lying flat on his back, his knees bent, his bare feet cocked up in the air making lazy circles as the pain tore at the wound through his bowels.

He'd undressed down to his long johns, raised the curtain on the far side, and slipped down behind the wagon wheel with the carbine.

The gray-white of his underwear was stained with yellow and red mixing together and puddling the ground.

Cadwell leaned over, looked at the bloody shoulder that had taken my first ricochet, and said, "I'll get my bag."

I knelt on the ground beside the lion of the prairie, feeling my own pain biting with barbed teeth into my side, and muttered, "I warned you not to . . ."

He stared at me and gasped, trying to make a last word or phrase.

"Not here . . ." I thought he said.

Staring up at the sky, he tried to make the old, cheery, man-to-man smile as he met his maker, starting his negotiations, perhaps, and he whispered, "Arlington for me . . ."

I thought about what it would cost the taxpayers to have him embalmed and put in a bronze casket, sent on a special railroad car with a company of cavalrymen a couple thousand miles back to Arlington, then the full-dress funeral with a chaplain and somebody important—maybe the new Assistant Secretary of War—giving the eulogy and placing the wreath, and I thought, I reckon you're going to stay right here.

The doctor returned a minute too late, and Barr staggered back to his chair, coughing hoarsely into a damp bandanna.

"Maybe you'd take a look at my side," I said, hanging onto the wagon wheel. "He's past help."

The doctor surprised me. He hadn't fainted yet, and when he pulled my shirt away from my side ribs he didn't flinch either.

"This will sting a bit," he said, dumping a dose of carbolic acid on a cotton pad and swabbing out the gouge in my side until it was clean. Then he put an acid-soaked compress on it and wrapped it tight on the wound.

"Uh-huh . . ." I said grimly.

"What?"

"It does sting some," I said as I heard Skofer coming on the run.

The knoll had been policed, raked, and groomed so that there was nothing that might offend the practiced eye of the oncoming generals and politicians.

The cook and the orderlies grumbled to themselves as we made ourselves comfortable in the camp, what there was left of us. Not counting Skofer or me, our group had dwindled down to the lieutenant, Sarah, the doctor, and Barr, who looked about as healthy as a leg of pickled mutton.

The corporal had been summoned on the double, and the burial detail quickly dug a grave back of the markers. Root, wrapped in a blanket, was quickly interred and covered over. There were no markers left, and the lieutenant thought it was just as well not to disturb the symmetry of the fours six deep.

The view from the knoll was a scene of serene tranquility except for Joe Minelli tearing down his scaffolding.

Over by the river the troopers polished their grays with pine-tar–soaked rags.

The pyramid on top of the monument looked like it might last as long as the pharaohs' in far-off Egypt. The bright new flag flew at half mast above it. Directly behind it was the general's grave, centered in front of the twenty-four crosses. One could imagine the general on a big gray horse leading a company of skeletal troopers in fours across the prairie.

Far to the northeast I saw a smudge of dust that ought to be the entourage of famous men, past, present, and future, marching this way to honor their fallen comrades.

"Think Minelli will make it in time?" I asked the lieutenant, who was nervously pacing back and forth.

"Unless he breaks a leg or something," Lieutenant

Falls said, "but how in blazes can I explain that Root is dead and there will be no oration?"

"Simply report it to General Sheridan as a fact. Disagreeable, but facts are facts."

"But the eulogy!" The lieutenant batted his fists together in frustration. "They'll want all the pomp and circumstances."

"I'll write a new one," Barr said. "Something brief but to the point, and you can read it."

The lieutenant looked at Barr, then at Sarah, a question in his eyes.

"It's the only way," she said firmly. "You can do it."

Barr took a notebook and the silver-mounted pen and ink case from inside his frock coat and sat at the big mess table, putting out the little inkwell and affixing a new steel nib into the penholder.

Without speaking he commenced writing smoothly, as if he had the whole speech already made up in his head.

When he felt a coughing fit coming on he carefully laid aside the pen and covered his mouth with a bandanna held in his left hand.

The doctor sat beside him but had no panacea to offer.

"I suppose you want your reward," the lieutenant said in a hushed voice, as if he might disturb Barr's train of thought.

"What do you think?" I countered.

"I wanted some evidence that would show beyond a shadow of a doubt who murdered my father."

"That's a problem, all right." I nodded. "There's no eyewitness except for Snow, and he never had time to talk about it."

"Then there is really no proof that Root was the man," the lieutenant said.

"Root tried to bushwhack me because I could ruin him." I nodded. "It's still wide open—Root, you, Doc Cadwell, and Mr. Barr."

"And me," Sarah Duffy said.

"If you want on the list, you're welcome," I said.

"She couldn't possibly have had the strength!" The lieutenant glared at me and moved protectively toward her.

"I scratched her off a long time ago," I said. "Now, if you'd just show me some evidence that you're perfectly innocent, I'll scratch you off, too."

"You can't believe I would butcher my own father!" the lieutenant said, his eyes burning.

"It isn't what I believe, but what the evidence proves," I said quietly. "I believe you said you checked the sentries on the nights the general and Snow were killed."

"Not just those two nights. I check every night," Lieutenant Falls said. "I would not post a reward for the capture of myself, either."

"You might if you thought it'd lead me away on another track," I murmured, glancing over at a frowning Skofer.

"There should have been blood on someone," Skofer said, "but we found no cast-off bloody clothing."

197

"I have only one spare uniform, and you've seen that," the lieutenant said with some relief.

"Why couldn't the killer have put on a rain slicker first, knowing there'd be blood spattered all over," Skofer put in.

"My raincape is spotless," the lieutenant snapped, then he turned to watch the dust cloud as it drew closer.

"Let's just say that's enough to let you out for now," I said, wanting to finish before meeting the government Goliaths. "If anybody knows anything about blood spattering around from severed arteries, it would be the doctor."

"Yes, there would be quite a lot," Doctor Cadwell said, nodding. "Not, of course, if he had received a lethal wound to the brain first, but the brain was undamaged."

"In fact, he died of loss of blood," I said, "almost at the same time his neck bones were severed."

"It's in my report," the doctor said, patting his silken curls.

"And next morning, down by the river, were you disposing of some clothing?"

"I had spilled some muriatic acid on my suit the day before," the doctor replied quickly. "It was hopelessly ruined."

"Did anybody see it happen?"

"I did." Barr stopped writing and gazed over at me.

"All right, say that's true." I nodded as Barr went back to his writing. "You certainly had reason enough to kill him."

198

"Everyone did," the doctor said. "Even you. The picture of that sergeant knocking you down to your knees will remain in my memory for a long time."

"We can get on to me later on," I said. "Right now we're tryin' to prove you're the guilty party."

"Believe me, if I wanted to kill him, I'd have used a poison so that he suffered enough to beg forgiveness," the doctor said, his face flushing with anger. "Strychnine administered intravenously with a syringe would have made a proper ending for him."

"But you'd have to knock him out first," I said.

"He was comatose from alcohol." The doctor spread his hands wide. "By the time he felt the needle it would have been too late."

"It sounds like you had it all planned out."

"As a matter of fact, I did. Despite my Hippocratic oath I was determined to rid the world of the bully."

"Did you pack up your syringe and go over to the general's ambulance?"

He hesitated, and it showed.

"What difference does it make now? He was not killed by poison."

"I was wondering if you happened to see anyone over there."

Again he hesitated, then said, "Don't try to put me someplace where I wasn't. I never left the daugherty."

"You said you saw Root leave that night . . ." I kept after him.

"Yes," he said, looking at the ground and stroking his long curls, "yes."

"You stick with that?" I kept on pushing.

"Yes," he sighed tiredly. "Yes."

"Did anyone else leave?"

"The lieutenant did as he said. I was asleep before he returned."

"You're going over old ground and getting nowhere," the lieutenant said sharply. His nervousness was getting progressively worse as the plume of dust lifted on the prairie and the sun stood almost overhead to mark the coming noon.

"We have plenty of time," I said. "They won't be here for another hour at least."

"I have a strong hunch," Skofer piped up, "that Sheridan and the senators and the rest of the heavyweights will not be coming."

"Why would they not come to honor my father?" the lieutenant asked coldly.

"They know he's dead. They're trained to avoid anything messy."

"Then who is coming?" The lieutenant looked dumbfounded.

"Probably a couple aides-de-camp, a gold-braided adjutant, a staff of lower-echelon polecats to decorate the occasion. The politicians will send underlings like Root."

"Then this really doesn't make much difference," Barr said, looking up at the lieutenant.

"It's got to be done to finish it all off, no matter who comes," the lieutenant said strongly. "It's what we do now that's important, not what they do."

"I agree," Barr said hoarsely, his voice clogging in his throat, and he went back to writing.

"I want to finish as much as any of you," I said heavily, and I whacked my hat against my leg in frustration. "Here we are, practically old friends, and one of you three is a killer. Why don't you just quit shielding one another and give me a straight answer?"

No one spoke until Sarah said, "There goes Mr. Minelli."

I looked down toward the monument and saw Joe Minelli had loaded the scaffolding on his wagon and was whipping his team across the prairie at a hard trot.

"He's not going to say good-bye."

"No," the lieutenant said, "I talked to him this morning. He'll put his uncle in touch with me, I think. Anyway, I paid him off, and he's leaving America."

"You don't think there's a chance he's the killer?" Skofer asked.

"No, I don't," the lieutenant said, "even if he had the strongest reason, more than any of us. I think he was just another one that arrived a little too late."

I looked down at the perfectly made memorial cemetery, the flag flying on the prairie wind, the bronze halyard swivel chiming against the iron pole making a cadence for the wind's lament, and I thought, it's a show put on by professional showmen, and nobody's coming to see it.

A sickening emptiness drained my strength as I pictured what it had been once, a traditional winter camp for the Kiowa, the decorated teepees, squaws dressing out buffalo robes, kids playing tag, warriors tightening arrowheads on their shafts.

The flag of the United States and the white flag of peace, both gifts of the general, proudly declaring the safekeeping of the village, then at daybreak . . . I thought of my own Arapahoe sweetheart in Colorado a million years ago when I'd left to go fight for the South. I thought of her and the baby caught in a similar surprise attack, nothing different, except it was the Colorado Volunteers that did it. Kill, rape, pillage, keep the prettiest maidens for the officers . . . nothing changes . . .

"Sam . . ."

I shook my head and saw Skofer's face in front of my staring eyes.

"Sam, you ready to go?"

"Hell, no!" I said angrily, shaking the pieces of the past out of my head. "We're not leaving till we're finished."

"Pity," Barr said, without stopping his smooth Spencerian script.

The doctor stood next to Skofer, looking at my bandage. "You may have lost more blood than I thought," he said.

"I slip off sometimes when I'm reminded of something that happened a long time ago," I said, mad at myself. I hadn't slipped like that for a year and a half. "It's like a bad dream that keeps coming back."

"We all have them," the lieutenant said.

"Odd, isn't it," Skofer said, "how some wounds never heal?"

"We must be careful," the doctor said quietly.

I wondered what that meant. Who was he talking to, and what had we to be careful about? Me? I didn't want to be careful. Life's not for the careful. Death is careful, it never takes a chance, is never beaten. I wondered then if anything ever changed. We had been all different types of people when we'd first arrived, and now half of us were dead and gone, and yet from somewhere would come the same type of people, the same looks, same smiles, same frowns, same worries, same ambitions, same faiths, same everything . . . it would just be different bodies. Even the bodies wouldn't be much different; maybe it would be only the names that were changed.

There was another overbearing, corrupt hulk growing up somewhere to replace the general. There was a halfbreed and a somewhat disappointed professor of divinity . . . we weren't really anything more than copies of somebody else to be copied again as death replaced us with others exactly the same. Our bodies would pass away, but not our style and outlook. Maybe that's what was meant by immortality. Somehow it didn't seem to work for my Arapahoe wife. I'd never seen anyone like her before or since.

"Sam," Skofer said again.

I looked around, saw them all looking at me like I was a bare-assed orangutan, and said, "I think I know it all, but I won't have time to prove it."

"Are you sure, Mr. Benbow?" Sarah asked, concern in her voice.

"It's easy for an old bloodhound," I muttered

tiredly. "I was just hopin' you'd all tell it straight and quit protecting him. Skofer, fetch me Snow's blouse, please."

Skofer was looking at me, frowning, worried, but I knew I hadn't lost that much blood. I'd just been flayed alive by lies from clever people, lies that weren't offered for greed or gain but to simply smooth the way for a decent dying.

Skofer put the leather tunic on the table near Barr's writing hand. I laid it out with the back up.

"This morning those two stains didn't look right. They still don't," I said.

"Must have lain on some chokecherries or something like that," the doctor said.

"There hasn't been a chokecherry or any kind of berry around here since July," I said. "No, he didn't lie down on anything, and you know it, Doctor."

"What is it, then?" the lieutenant asked, coming close and scratching at one of the splotches with his fingernail. "It couldn't be blood, because the wire never cut the skin . . ."

"That's right, Lieutenant," I said, moving off to the front of the knoll where I could look out over the vast pristine prairie.

"It couldn't be, but it is. I've seen enough blood to know it, and I don't need any fancy tests to prove it. So whose blood is it?"

"Holy Mother of God," Sarah said softly, her eyes fixed on Barr as he broke into a hard, hacking cough. His features contorted, his mouth hidden by a folded-up bandanna to catch the bright spots of blood coming up from his lungs.

"You knew it all along," the doctor said reproachfully.

"The only explanation for these blood spots is that Barr couldn't cover his mouth while he was strangling a very strong man."

Barr stared at me, nodded, took a rasping breath, then carefully put a period at the end of his sentence.

"But you don't know why, do you?" he asked softly, as if he were admitting he'd lost a race, but only because he'd come in second.

"You killed Snow because he'd found that pen case in the general's ambulance after you lost it swinging the battle axe," I said. "Everyone mentioned stolen articles except you. Snow wanted something for that pen case or he was going to tell me what he'd seen and found."

"Drat the luck." Barr smiled. "He made all kinds of problems for me. Hard to handle, too. Something in my chest broke from gripping the wire."

"Why did you kill my father?" Lieutenant Falls asked weakly. "Just because he raked you over the coals?"

"No, no," Barr said hoarsely, his white face highlighted by the rosy red spots on his cheeks like a Punch-and-Judy clown's face, tragic and happy, changing back and forth. "I was used to that."

His throat clogged, and he was hammered by the racking cough. When he finally sucked in a little air he smiled, his eyes wet, and said, "No, it was the announcement of his promotion. All along over the years I'd thought there would be an end to him. But with his being put in charge of eliminating the Sioux, which could only lead on to the presidency, I thought, Well, Gerald, you've not done anything with your life yet, why don't you do something worthwhile before it's too late?"

"Rest, Gerald," Doc Cadwell said worriedly.

Barr waved a lazy hand. "There will be no paintings, no poems, nothing but the easily forgotten drivel that, as you said, made a silk purse out of a sow's ear."

As the next attack hit him he pushed the page toward the lieutenant and whispered, "Go ahead, practice your speech."

The lieutenant glanced over at Sarah, and she nodded. He looked down at Barr, who had laid his head down on his right arm, sucking in air in short, quick breaths.

"On this infamous anniversary we speak truly for all those who died here a year ago. Except perhaps for the innocent children, they were as brave as anyone in the face of death. Beyond any of the dead's comprehension, the cause was contrived and managed by ambitious men with withered manhood and corrupted ideals. Pity the children; nothing was gained except our shame that burns like winter ice. Let this monument then mark a conspired encounter of the Iron Age with the Stone Age, which history will record as a tragic defeat for each and every one of us."

Sucking for air, I saw Barr's shoulders convulse and

heard a shriek of fear tear from his throat as something ripped loose in his chest. A gout of flowing bright-red blood filled his mouth and stopped his throat.

The doctor quickly grabbed him and held him in his arms until the little kicks and spasms and quiverings dwindled away, and we had another body to bury.

— 14 —

THE PLUME OF DUST WASN'T BIG ENOUGH FOR AN ENTOU-rage of surreys, daughertys, buggies, stagecoaches, or even Conestoga wagons.

"Scouts?" the lieutenant asked.

I looked at Skofer and shook my head.

"Let's wait and see," I said.

There was no cloud of dust following the four riders in blue as they approached the knoll.

On the shoulder straps of the one on the left were two bars. The other was a sergeant. Riding behind were Sergeant Price and a Company B corporal.

Without dismounting the captain saluted Lieutenant Falls and said, "Captain Stanton with orders to relieve you, sir."

"Please step down, Captain," Falls said.

Captain Stanton turned to his sergeant and said, "Strike the camp and prepare to march."

"Yes, sir." The sergeant saluted, gestured to Price and the corporal, and rode off toward Company B.

Satisfied that his orders would be carried out, Captain Stanton dismounted and looked us over. The camp was clean. There was no more clotted blood on the table. There was no sign of a hastily dug grave down below by the monument.

"I don't understand, sir," Lieutenant Falls said stiffly.

"These are your orders, Lieutenant," Stanton said, handing over a blue envelope. "You are being transferred from the Fifth to the Ninth Cavalry at Fort Sill."

"Buffalo soldiers . . ." Lieutenant Falls nodded. "Guard duty. Nothing to do and nowhere to go."

"You know the army," Captain Stanton said levelly.

"May I ask about the orders for Company B?"

"I'm to join General Crook with Company B as soon as possible at Fort Hays. General Custer has been selected to spearhead the pacification of the Sioux. We will support him."

"You mean they've already picked Custer as their golden champion?" Falls smiled and shook his head. "My father's been dead less than a week."

"We can only wonder and follow orders," Captain Stanton said with a trace of sympathy in his tone.

"When will General Sheridan and his entourage arrive?" the lieutenant asked.

Jack Curtis

"They are not coming. He and his staff are concentrating on the campaign against the Sioux. Time is critical."

"I know . . ." Lieutenant Falls nodded. "An election coming up . . ."

"You mean no one is coming for the ceremony?" I asked. "Not even a congressman?"

"I was informed there will be no ceremony until a later time, perhaps next year. General Sheridan believes it can wait."

I smiled and looked at Skofer and said, "You called it."

"Captain Stanton," Lieutenant Falls said, "on your return, would you please forward this letter of resignation? I'm just interested in commanding myself."

"You know, sir," the captain said coldly, "that if you finish with the army, the army is finished with you."

"That only holds true until they need men to fight." Lieutenant Falls smiled, and his shoulders came back like he'd just shucked off the weight of ages.

"Miss Duffy," I said, taking her strong hand, "we'll be sayin' good-bye, and I hope you don't have any hard feelin's."

"No hard feelings, Sam." Sarah smiled. "You're just too much man for a country schoolteacher."

"Maybe a young fellow that wants to get a fresh start in California might be a better companion," I said.

"You have a way of reading my mind." She blushed.

210

"About the reward money," Falls said, joining us.
"I can mail it to you."

"Care of the South Texas Cattlemen's Association,
Austin, Texas," Skofer put in quickly.

"Golly! It feels so good to be free!" the lieutenant
blurted out, laughing crazily. "Come see us out in San
Juan Bautista."

"We aim to do just that," Skofer said.

The prairie wind mourned over the hill and tolled
the bronze ring against the flagpole in a dismal,
monotonous pealing, singing its own unfailing elegy
for the changing prairie.

Moving off the crest of the knoll, I heard the
Company B bugler blow "Boots and Saddles," and a
minute later Skofer commenced screeching louder
than the wind and bugle combined:

"I'll go back to Texas and stay there a year,
Instead of cold water my drink will be beer . . ."

He paused a moment, looked down at the graveyard
by the river, sighted off at the gray western horizon,
and shook his head. When he resumed, his voice was
soft and thoughtful, harmonizing with the wind, bless-
ing the ignoble but still tragic scene the only way he
could:

"And when I return, a new man in the spring,
I will see the waters glide and hear the nightin-
    gales sing . . ."

Jack Curtis was born at Lincoln Center, Kansas. At an early age he came to live in Fresno, California. He served in the U.S. Navy during the Second World War, with duty in the Pacific theater. He began writing short stories after the war for the magazine market. Sam Peckinpah, later a film director, had also come from Fresno, and he enlisted Curtis in writing teleplays and story adaptations for *Dick Powell's Zane Grey Theater*. Sometimes Curtis shared credit for these teleplays with Peckinpah; sometimes he did not. Other work in the television industry followed with Curtis writing episodes for *The Rifleman*, *Have Gun, Will Travel*, Sam Peckinpah's *The Westerner*, *Rawhide*, *The Outlaws*, *Wagon Train*, *The Big Valley*, *The Virginian* and *Gunsmoke*. Curtis also contributed teleplays to non-Western series like *Dr. Kildare*, *Ben Casey* and *Four Star Theater*. He lives on a ranch in Big Sur, California, with his wife, LaVon. In recent years Jack Curtis published numerous books of poetry, wrote *Christmas in Calico* (1996) that was made into a television movie, and numerous Western novels, including *Lie, Eliza, Lie* (2002), *Pepper Tree Rider* (1994) and *No Mercy* (1995).

BRANCH	DATE
Ey	1/1